Maui Madness

By

Kathi Daley

D1470453

This book is a work of fiction. Names, characters, places, and incidents either are products of the author's imagination or are used fictitiously. Any resemblance to actual events or locales or persons, living or dead, is entirely coincidental.

Copyright © 2014 by Katherine Daley

Version 1.0

All rights reserved, including the right of reproduction in whole or in part in any form.

This book is dedicated to a very special MOM from my teenage years, Bernadette Wheeler. She was a very special woman who was loved by many and will be missed.

Special thanks to all my Facebook friends who show their support by sharing their opinions and encouragement. I also want to thank my team of advance readers for taking time out of their busy lives to help me launch each new book.

And, as always, love and thanks to my sister Christy for her time, encouragement, unwavering support, and valuable feedback. I also want to thank Carrie, Cristin, and Danny for the Facebook shares, Ricky for the webpage, Randy Ladenheim-Gil for the editing, and, last but not least, my super-husband Ken for allowing me time to write by taking care of everything else.

Books by Kathi Daley

Paradise Lake Series:
Pumpkins in Paradise
Snowmen in Paradise
Bikinis in Paradise

Zoe Donovan Mysteries:
Halloween Hijinks
The Trouble With Turkeys
Christmas Crazy
Cupid's Curse
Big Bunny Bump-off
Beach Blanket Barbie
Maui Madness
Derby Divas – coming July 2014

Road to Christmas Romance:
Road to Christmas Past

Chapter 1

Thursday, June 26

There are some things you should never do.

Not even if you *are* on vacation and you adhere to the adage what happens in Maui stays in Maui.

Not even if you're able to make your boyfriend laugh and your best friends smile for the first time in weeks.

Not even if you're sipping your third Mai Tai in less than two hours and any inhibitions you may have at one point possessed have gone the way of your common sense.

Unfortunately, I didn't stumble across this very important piece of insight until it was too late. Much, much too late.

"They're almost ready for you," the woman who poured me into a bikini at least a size too small assured me.

"Are you sure you don't have a larger bikini top?" I desperately tried one last time.

"Don't worry; you look great," the gaudily clad woman dressed in leopard-print tights and a tube top assured me.

"To be honest, at this point I'm much less concerned about looking great than I am about one or both of the girls making a guest appearance before the end of the show." I looked down at my breasts, which looked ready to explode from the top, which must have been designed to fit a prepubescent twelve-year-old.

The woman laughed. "Don't worry. That hardly ever happens."

Terrific.

I glanced out at the audience, who were being entertained by the antics of our host, Hula Bob (yes, he actually calls himself that). I figured the effects of the Mai Tai must be wearing off because it suddenly occurred to me how absurd the series of events leading up to this moment really were.

It all started a mere five days ago. My boyfriend, Zak Zimmerman, and my best friends, Ellie Davis and Levi Denton, had all suffered painful losses, so we'd decided—quite spontaneously, I might add—to fly to Hawaii for the two weeks Ellie was supposed to be on her Hawaiian honeymoon. It made perfect sense at the time. The beach house Zak had borrowed for Ellie's honeymoon was already reserved; Ellie had arranged to take the time off from work; Levi, a teacher, was off for the summer; and I had wonderful assistants to cover for me at the animal rescue and rehabilitation shelter I run. Zak, of course, is stinking rich and works when he wants to.

With barely a thought, we'd packed our bags and flown across the ocean on the private jet Zak had chartered so that my dog Charlie could come along.

The thing is, as spontaneous and fun as I found the adventure, Zak, Levi, and Ellie barely said a word on the flight over or the limo ride to the house. I had felt bad for my friends and wanted so desperately for them to have a wonderful time that when I saw the flyer announcing tonight's comedy show, I'd begged, prodded, bribed, and pleaded until the gang agreed to go.

"Two minutes," the woman whispered as I fought the urge to flee.

The show really had been funny to this point, and we'd arrived early, so we had perfect seats right in the front. Hula Bob had a tendency to find the absurd in everyday life that most of the audience found quite comical. I could see that my friends were beginning to relax and have fun for the first time in weeks, and I guess I got caught up in the festive atmosphere. Still, I'm not sure that explains the brief moment of insanity that caused me to jump onto my feet and raise both hands high into the air when Hula Bob asked for a volunteer from the audience.

How bad could it be? I'd reasoned as I'd jumped up and down, yelling "Pick me, pick me."

"Ready?" The woman with the leopard-print tights took my hand and led me onto the stage.

"Ladies and gentlemen," Hula Bob announced, "let's put our hands together for our final volunteer, Zoe Donovan."

Everyone clapped and quite a few of the men whistled as I was led onto the stage in nothing but the very small bikini. I tried to smile and look at the audience but couldn't help but glance down at Thelma and Louise to verify that they were staying put.

As I walked onto the stage in my bare feet, I saw that there were three other women dressed pretty much the same as me. They looked happy and relaxed. Perhaps they knew something I didn't.

"So tell me, Ms. Donovan," Bob said, turning on the charm, "would you say that you're a good sport?"

Uh-oh.

I wanted to say no, but then I glanced at Zak, who had a huge smile on his face. God, I love that smile. I've missed it so much in the weeks since Lambda had his fall.

"You bet I'm a good sport." I turned on my brightest smile.

"Fantastic." Bob grinned. "Did the women backstage tell you what it is you volunteered for?"

"They said I was going to be a contestant in a series of games and if I won, I would receive a prize package filled with gift cards for area restaurants and events, including," I grinned at Zak and Levi, "two passes to the dive event at the Maui Ocean Center."

Zak and Levi both let out a whoop-whoop. The men had wanted to participate in the dive event, but the slots were limited and had been sold out for months.

"Okay, let's get started." The silver buttons on Bob's bright yellow suit glistened in the overhead lights. "The four of you will compete in three events. The winner of each event will be given three points, the runner-up will be given two, the woman in third place will get one point, and the woman in last place will receive none. Whoever has the most total points at the end wins the gift basket."

Sounded straightforward. None of the other women looked to be in as good shape as I am, so I figured I had this locked in.

"Our first event is titled Diving for Bootie. You'll each be given a list of five things to dive for. The first one to recover all five wins the event."

I supposed that explained the swimsuit. I was both a scuba diver and a free diver and had been on the dive team in high school, so I figured that whichever type of dive Hula Bob was referring to, I had this event in the bag. I was feeling self-confident to the point of smugness when the stagehands rolled out four Dumpsters filled with garbage.

"We're diving in those?" I groaned.

"Do you see a pool?" Hula Bob asked, his white teeth shining like a beacon in contrast to his deeply tanned face.

I wishfully looked around. "No, I guess not."

Hula Bob handed us each a piece of paper. On the list were five items. Bob explained that each Dumpster contained the five items and our task was to hop on in and start digging until we found all five. I was about to refuse until I noticed that the other three women trotted over to their Dumpsters and began stretching like they were preparing for an Olympic event.

If they can do it, I can do it, I decided.

"I'll count down from three. When I say go, you can hop on in," Bob instructed.

I quickly looked at my list. Item number one was a diaper. *Ew.* I really, really hoped it was an unused diaper. I had a new baby sister and had certainly changed my share of *used* diapers as of late, but I really didn't want to land on one when I was launched into the Dumpster by the nice man who was assigned to give me a boost.

I'm not sure what exactly happened upon my entry to the Dumpster, but somehow I got turned around and ended up falling headfirst into the mess. I didn't even want to think about the squishy thing my head hit until I realized it was spaghetti, item number three.

Awesome. Only four items to go.

I managed to be the second person to climb out of her Dumpster with all five items. Sure, I had spaghetti in my hair and something green and disturbingly gooey on my left thigh, but I also had two points. I wasn't sure what the next two events would entail, but I was determined to win this thing or die trying.

"Can I get a round of applause for all four women?" Bob shouted into the microphone.

Everyone hooted and shouted out the name of their favorite contestant. I could tell that I was by far the fan favorite. I raised my hands in victory and danced around in such a way as to make Rocky proud. I was actually having a really good time until I heard the details of challenge number two.

"I can't believe you ate that whole thing," Levi commented as we walked back to the car after I'd showered and changed back into the clothes I'd arrived in.

"I wasn't going to, but the other women didn't seem to have a problem with it and I didn't want to be the only one to back out."

"The other women were part of the show. They were in on everything," Levi pointed out. "I'm pretty sure their black and chunky pie was chocolate pudding with nuts, not pig organs in God knows what."

"I know that now, but I didn't know that then," I argued. "You should have warned me."

"I wanted the dive tickets." Levi laughed.

I punched him in the arm.

Hard.

It turned out that while I'd eaten the worst-tasting thing I'd ever put in my mouth, sat in a variety of delightfully messy products, and gone diving in garbage—*real garbage*—the other women had only pretended to play along. There wasn't anything in their Dumpsters other than the items they were supposed to find, and I was pretty sure Levi was correct about the chocolate pudding. The whole thing had been fixed and the audience was in on it.

Apparently, my total degradation was hilarious.

I should be furious that my friends let me go through with the ruse, but I *had* volunteered and, truth be told, if I were in the audience watching as some other slightly drunk mainlander participated in dumb tourist tricks, I would have thought it was hilarious as well.

Still, I *had* gotten the coveted tickets for Zak and Levi, and the cloud of doom that seemed to have encompassed my friends for the past week apparently had been lifted. At least for the moment. All and all, I'd say it was an evening well spent.

"You know what my favorite part of the whole night was?" Levi asked as I walked beside him on the way to our car.

"What? The mashed potatoes in my butt crack?"

"Close." Levi laughed. One of the games was a sort of musical chairs in which one chair in each round had something gross on the seat. If it was the only seat left, you were forced to choose between sitting in it and forfeiting the game. It just *happened* to work out that I was standing in front of the gross chair every time.

"Actually, my favorite part was the photos I managed to take for my Facebook page."

"You didn't!" I growled as I grabbed for his cell phone.

"'Fraid so. The picture of you climbing out of the Dumpster with spaghetti in your hair already has two hundred likes and the shot of you turning green as you chocked down that black slop has gone viral. You'll be famous by morning."

"Take them down," I demanded as I tried to grab Levi's phone.

Levi held his phone over my head where I couldn't reach it.

"Zak, make him give me the phone," I insisted.

"Sorry, he's your friend." Zak laughed. "I try never to get between you and your friends."

"But it's humiliating," I wailed.

Zak stopped walking. He turned so that we were facing each other and tucked a stray lock of my still-wet hair behind my ear. "Actually," he began, "the sight of Louise peeking out of your bikini top while you climbed out of the Dumpster with green slime on your leg and pasta in your hair is the sexiest thing I've seen for a very long time."

"You are seriously deranged." I rolled my eyes.

Zak kissed me on the lips. "No, I'm just totally in love with this wonderful person who would go to so much effort to make sure that her friends are having a good time. You really are a uniquely awesome person, Zoe Donovan."

I wrapped my arms around Zak's neck and gave him a kiss. A real one.

"Get a room," Ellie teased.

That, I decided, was exactly what I was going to do.

Chapter 2

Friday, June 27

"So how's Hawaii?" Jeremy Fisher and Tiffany Middleton, my assistants at the animal control and rehabilitation shelter we run, asked in tandem during our first video conference since I'd arrived.

Jeremy snickered, so I figured he'd found Levi's photos online.

"Hawaii is great. We're having an excellent time," I responded.

"Taken in any good shows on the island?" Jeremy laughed out loud.

"Very funny." I stuck out my tongue at him.

"Seriously, that video of you doing the whole musical chairs thing left me lying on the floor in stitches. And the look on your face when you choked down the mud pie was hysterical. I'm thinking of freezing a few of the frames and printing portraits to hang in the lobby."

"If you do, you'll be looking for another job."

Jeremy obviously didn't take my threat seriously because he held up a photo of me climbing out of the Dumpster that he'd printed from Levi's Facebook photos. "Did they let you keep that bikini? Because it's really something."

"Leave Zoe alone." Tiffany kicked Jeremy. "Other than the comedy club and the momentary lapse in judgment when you volunteered to be a participant, how are you liking the house and the island?"

"It's so awesome." I smiled at Tiffany in gratitude for changing the subject. "Truly. Words cannot describe the awesomeness of this awesome island."

"That's a lot of awesome," Tiffany said.

"Seriously." I giggled. "The island is everything I dreamed it would be and the house is really gorgeous. Let me give you a tour."

I held up the computer, which featured a camera, and began to walk around the house on Maui's west shore that Zak's friend Keoke had let us use for two weeks. "This is the awesome living area." I showed my friends the large great room, which was open to the outside through huge glass doors in the wall. "When you roll back the glass wall, it's like having no wall at all," I said, demonstrating.

"Wow." Tiffany gasped in awe. "It must feel like you're sitting on an outdoor patio even though you're actually indoors."

"Yeah, it really does. You can sit in comfort while listening to the waves crash and enjoying a summer breeze. This is the seating area." The room featured multiple sofas, a top-notch entertainment center, and the best feature in the huge room, an enormous saltwater aquarium that displayed colorful fish that could be found in the ocean just steps from the back door.

"And it has a full kitchen?" Tiffany asked.

I walked toward the kitchen, which was open to the living area. "This is the dining table." I showed my coworkers a long table that could easily seat twenty. "And this is the kitchen."

"I love the granite countertops. And the appliances," Tiffany drooled. "You could cook for a lot of people in that kitchen."

"The owner uses it for corporate retreats as well as a family getaway, so no expense has been spared. The bedrooms are down this hall." I pointed the camera toward the hallway. "I won't go poking into everyone's private space, but each room has an ocean view and a private bathroom. Zak and I even have a Jacuzzi that's more than big enough for two."

"It looks like heaven on earth," Tiffany sighed.

"I haven't even shown you the best part." I walked the computer outside. "This is the pool area. As you can see, it's situated right on the ocean." It was a beautiful day, the sun shining down on the big waves that rolled onto a white sand beach. "There's a huge patio with a fire pit and an outdoor kitchen that's three times as large as my indoor kitchen at home."

"It's really beautiful," Jeremy commented.

I just glared at him.

"I'm sorry I teased you," he apologized, "and I really am glad that you're all having a good time. Forgive me?"

"Are you going to destroy the photos you printed?"

"Already done." Jeremy tore them in half.

"Okay, then I guess I forgive you."

"So other than the comedy club, tell me about your visit," Tiffany encouraged.

"I've been here less than forty-eight hours, but I'm already in love with the place." I set the computer on a table and sat down on one of the lounge chairs. The sun hitting my bare legs was warm in spite of the fact that it was still early in the morning. "I sat out here earlier and watched dolphins jumping in the distance as I drank my coffee. It was so peaceful and relaxing to listen to the waves crashing onto the beach. I understand if you come during the winter, you can see whales as well."

"I'd love to see whales," Tiffany gushed.

"Zak said they're regular visitors to the channel on this side of the island. I'm hoping I can convince him to bring me back during the winter."

"I'm sure Zak will do anything you want," Jeremy assured me. "Is that Molokai in the background?"

"Yes. How did you know?"

"The scenery you showed us looks similar to the landscape that was in the background when I saw a news report on that missing judge. The reporter mentioned that the island you could see in the distance was Molokai."

"Missing judge?" I asked.

"You didn't hear about that? It was all over the national news this past week," Jeremy informed me.

"I guess I haven't watched much television lately," I admitted. "I've been pretty distracted, getting everything taken care of that needed to be handled in order for me to be gone for two weeks."

"Some judge and two of his friends went sailing last weekend and never returned. There was a huge search, but they still haven't been found. It's quite the mystery because it was a bright, sunny day and the judge was an experienced sailor."

"Wow, how awful. Zak hasn't mentioned it, but then, he's had a lot on his mind."

"I'm sure you'll hear about it now that you're in the area. They've called off the search, but I imagine that a missing judge is a hot topic, and the manner in which he disappeared is pretty freaky. The reporter was camped out in front of the judge's house and the scenery in the background looked very similar to what I'm seeing now, so I'm betting he lives in the area where you're staying."

I had this sinking feeling in my gut. At times I can't even explain how I know things, but somehow I knew that before our time on the island was over, I'd somehow become involved in the saga of the missing judge and the boat that seemed to have disappeared into thin air.

"How is Charlie doing with the new atmosphere?" Tiffany asked.

I smiled, grateful for the change of topic. "He's taking everything in stride. Say hi," I said, pointing the camera at a padded lounge chair next to the pool where Charlie had been napping.

"Hi, Charlie," Jeremy and Tiffany both greeted him.

Charlie looked up as he tried to figure out where the voices were coming from.

"How did Charlie do on the flight over?" Tiffany asked.

"Really good, actually. Since Zak chartered a private jet, he was able to sit next to me and look out of the window for most of the journey. I thought the noise and confusion might frighten him, but he seemed to enjoy the experience. Once we landed, he followed Zak down the stairs onto the tarmac and hopped right into the limo that was waiting for us when directed to do so. How are Marlow and Spade?"

Tiffany had volunteered to stay at my boathouse while I was away to take care of the precious kitties in my life. I could have taken them over to my parents', but I knew that in the long run they'd be much happier at home, in a familiar environment, and Tiffany had assured me that she was thrilled to stay at my lakefront property.

"They're doing fine. Marlow has been testing his limits a bit since you've been gone, but I think we'll be able to come to an understanding."

"Uh-oh. What'd he do?" I asked. Marlow, my huge orange-and-white tabby, was by far the more active and mischievous of the two felines.

"Nothing serious. He just seemed to think it would be funny to empty the hamper and hide my clothes all over the house. I've looked and looked, but I'm still missing one sock and a bra."

"Don't feel bad; he does that to me at times. I think he gets bored being alone all day. It would seem Spade would be good company for him, but Spade is a lazy cat who likes to sleep all day, while Marlow likes to play. I've found the best remedy to the missing clothes situation is to keep the hamper in the bathroom and then keep the door closed while I'm gone."

"Have you thought about getting one of those towers that cats can climb and play on? Maybe Marlow just needs more exercise."

"I'm not sure where I'd put it. My boathouse is pretty small," I pointed out.

"I think my mom has one in her garage from a cat I had as a kid. She's coming to have lunch with me tomorrow. I'll ask her to bring it, and if Marlow likes it, we can work on somewhere to put it."

"Okay, that sounds like a good plan. So how are things at the Zoo?" I asked the question I'd called to find out in the first place.

"You've only been gone two days," Jeremy pointed out.

"I know, but Zak and Levi went fishing and Ellie decided to go for a walk, so I'm home alone with time to think, and I started wondering about the dead squirrels in the campground and the stray dog who has been terrorizing picnickers on the beach."

"You're at the house alone?" Tiffany asked without answering my question. "Why didn't you go fishing with the guys or walking with Ellie?"

"I didn't go with the guys because I hate fishing, and Ellie seemed like she wanted to be alone with her thoughts. It was such a hectic few days getting ready to make the trip that I tend to forget it's only been a week since Rob broke her heart."

"How *is* she doing?" Jeremy asked.

I sighed. "Honestly, I'm not sure. She was really quiet on the trip over, but she seemed to loosen up last night while I humiliated myself in front of hundreds of total strangers. She laughed with everyone else and really looked like she was having a good time. I thought things were going to be okay, but then she came out of her room this morning looking like she hadn't slept at all. She said she needed to think, so I decided to give her some space."

"The poor thing is taking this breakup really hard," Tiffany sympathized.

"She really is," I agreed. "I honestly feel that what happened was the best thing for everyone involved, but I hate to see Ellie go through this. I know how much she loves Hannah, and how much she was looking forward to being her mother, but I can't help but feel happy that Hannah and her real mother have been reunited."

For those of you who might have missed the Ellie-and-Rob saga, Rob is Ellie's ex-fiancé and Hannah is his daughter. Rob had been raising his daughter on his own until Ellie came along and fell in love with the toddler. When Rob's father passed away, Rob went back to his hometown for the funeral and ran into Hannah's mother. When Hannah had been born, Cassie hadn't wanted to take on the responsibility of a child, so she'd left the infant with Rob, but in the past two years she'd had time to think about her choices, and the two decided to reunite. Rob had called Ellie and broken off their engagement over the phone.

"Rob is in town," Jeremy informed me. "I guess he's planning to pack up and be gone by the time you guys get back. I noticed he's put his house up for sale."

"I think that's for the best. Is Hannah with him?"

"Yes," Jeremy answered. "And Cassie is with him as well."

"I'm glad Ellie isn't there. It would be so hard for her to see Hannah with Cassie. Hopefully, by the time we get home, Ellie will be in a mental space where she can put this behind her and get on with her life."

"And Levi?" Tiffany asked.

Levi had suffered his own personal trauma when his ex had been murdered in May.

"He seems to be doing okay. I think he still feels bad that he wasn't able to help Barbie, but if I had to guess, I'd say he's decided to deal with his feelings and enjoy the trip. Keoke not only let us borrow the house but the boat, jet skis, and a storage shed full of surfboards and kayaks as well."

"And Zak?" Tiffany wondered.

Zak's dog Lambda had died after a lifetime of medical challenges resulting from being attacked by a bear when he was young.

"He's okay. He misses Lambda, of course. The fall shortened his time with us, but we all knew Lambda had been going downhill for some time. Charlie has been really great. He seems to know that Zak needs a little extra TLC and jumps into his lap every time he sees him."

"How about you?" Jeremy teased. "Have you been spending time in his lap as well?"

"Wouldn't you like to know?" I grinned into the camera. "It's early yet, but I thought I might talk to Zak about another dog when we get back home. I hate to think of him alone in that huge house."

"You do realize that if you, Charlie, and the cats move in with Zak, he won't be alone in his big house," Tiffany said.

"So back to the dead squirrels and the nuisance dog," I changed the subject. It wasn't that I never wanted to take things to the next level with Zak; it was more that I wasn't ready to make such a permanent decision quite yet. I'd known Zak since the seventh grade, but we'd been dating for less than a year. "Any updates?"

"According to the forest service, they don't know why squirrels are turning up dead. They don't seem to have any identifiable diseases, but three more were found yesterday. They've sent the carcasses out for additional testing. In the meantime, we posted signs warning residents and visitors to stay away from them and to call us if they find additional victims."

"And the dog?"

Jeremy hesitated. He looked at Tiffany and she shrugged. Jeremy looked back toward the camera as if trying to make a decision.

"The dog?" I asked again.

"He's dead," Jeremy said. "I found him this morning when I went to retrieve the dead squirrels. We think that with the addition of the dog, poison may be causing the squirrel deaths rather than disease. An autopsy on the dog might provide additional information."

I never wanted to hear that a dog had suffered a premature death even if the dog in question was a stray that was terrorizing campers. But poisoning? That was bad news all around.

"You need to let everyone know that a poisoning danger may exist," I insisted. "Not just those staying in the campground but all pet owners in the area."

"Tiffany and I wanted to print up flyers and run an ad in the paper, but the county wants to wait until we get the test results back," Jeremy informed me. "They feel that advertising the fact that we've had a rash of dead squirrels that may have contracted some sort of disease is bad enough, but if we alert the public to a threat of potential poisoning for any dog that happens along, it will cause a panic."

"You can't wait," I insisted. "Better to cause a panic and then have to recant if we were premature than to have another victim. Make up the flyers. If the county has a problem with them, tell them to call me. I have my cell."

"Okay," Jeremy agreed.

"Maybe I'll call Salinger and fill him in. It's starting to sound like more is going on than we first believed. If someone is intentionally poisoning animals, the sheriff will want to know."

"I can call Salinger," Jeremy said. "You're supposed to be on vacation, not dealing with all of this."

"If someone is leaving poison out for animals to find, I want to be involved with bringing him or her down. Don't worry; I still plan to enjoy the trip. We're all going to go to an authentic luau tomorrow. It's a private party being thrown by Keoke's grandparents. Keoke's cousin just got engaged to some guy, so they're throwing a party to celebrate."

"Keoke is the man who owns the house you're staying in?" Jeremy clarified.

"Yeah. He lives on Oahu but spends a lot of time on Maui. I'm really excited. Zak said there are going to be hula dancers and fire twirlers. They're roasting a pig and everything."

"Ew." Tiffany grimaced. "A whole pig?"

"Yeah, *ew* was my first reaction as well, but I decided that while I'm on the island, I'm going to embrace the culture. I mean, it can't be any worse than the black goop I ate last night. And since I've already gotten past that first awkward moment when you truly humiliate yourself, I might even try my hand—or perhaps I should say my hips—at the hula."

"Be sure to have someone film it 'cause this I have to see." Jeremy laughed. "It might even get more hits than your musical-chairs video."

"Very funny," I shot back.

"Are you going to wear a grass skirt?" Tiffany asked.

"I have a Hawaiian print skirt and a matching halter top that should do the trick. Zak and Levi bought Hawaiian shirts to go with shorts they brought from home."

"And Ellie?" Tiffany asked.

"Ellie keeps saying she might just stay home with Charlie, but I'm going to try to convince her to go. If she does, I have a colorful skirt that would look nice on her. I hate to have her miss all the fun, but I know how it is when you just want to sit quietly and heal. I've decided I'm going to encourage and support but not push."

"That sounds like a good plan," Tiffany agreed.

"Oh, before I forget to ask you," Jeremy added, "the Bryton Lake shelter wants us to take seven of their short-timers. We have room, but the problem is that their facility has recently experienced a pretty severe case of kennel cough. The quarantine has been lifted, but *just* lifted, so I thought I should run it by you first. I know how contagious that is, and I wouldn't want any of our dogs to get sick."

"Tell them we'll take them, but have Scott look at them right away. If he feels that any of the dogs have symptoms, isolate them. In fact, it might be a good idea to keep all the new dogs together and away from the others. You can use the large animal yard to exercise them since we don't currently have any large cats in residence. I'd wait to adopt them out until we've had them for a few days and can be sure they are unaffected."

"Okay. I'll call Scott and set it up."

"It sounds like Ellie is back, so I guess I'll sign off, but call me if you find out anything more about the dead dog and squirrels. I'll call Salinger as soon as I'm finished here. And don't let the county bully you about the flyers warning people of a possible danger from poisoning. If they have a problem with our proactive approach, they can call me."

"Don't worry. We can handle it," Jeremy assured me. "You just have fun and enjoy your time off. It'll be over before you know it and you'll wish you could have relaxed while you had the chance."

"Yeah, you're right, and I trust both of you to handle whatever comes up. You know me, though; I like to be in the middle of things. It never has been easy for me to sit on the sidelines."

"This is a good chance for you to work on that," Tiffany encouraged. "Give Ellie a hug for me and say hi to Zak and Levi. Hopefully, they won't bring home a bunch of fish that need cleaning. It'd be a shame to stink up that beautiful kitchen."

"If they have fish, they can stay in the outdoor kitchen until it's time to eat them," I assured her. "Oh, and can one of you call my dad and mom and tell them to keep their dogs away from the campground? I'll be unavailable all day tomorrow, but I'll talk to you both the day after that."

"That'll be Sunday, so we'll be closed," Jeremy reminded me. "I think Tank is on for the overnight shift and Gunnar is going to check in on things during the day."

Tiffany elbowed Jeremy. "I'll come in. Call me at around nine our time and I'll be here to give you an update."

I smiled. "Thanks. I'll owe you."

Chapter 3

After I hung up with Jeremy and Tiffany, I went in search of Ellie, who I was sure I'd heard come in through the front door. I found her on the patio, talking to a young girl who looked to be native Hawaiian. She had a petite frame, a dark complexion, and straight black hair that hung past her waist. She was dressed in cutoff shorts and a bright orange tank top and looked to be no older than sixteen.

"Zoe, this is Malie," Ellie introduced us. "I ran into her while on my walk and we got to talking."

"I'm glad to meet you," I said.

"Malie works for an organization that monitors and preserves the sea turtles and other wildlife in the area. I happened to see a turtle on the beach while I was walking and went to take a closer look. Malie was working in the area and stopped to talk. I mentioned that you owned your own foundation that rescues and rehabilitates animals native to the area where we live, and we realized that the two of you would have a lot in common, so I invited her to lunch."

"I'd love to talk with you about the work you do." I smiled at the exotic young woman, who must be older than I'd first assumed. "I was just about to look for something to make for lunch, so the timing is perfect. We stopped at Costco yesterday, so we're well stocked. What would you like?"

"I enjoy all types of food," Malie said.

"My stomach is a bit topsy-turvy," Ellie admitted. "I guess I didn't sleep all that well last night. Probably jet lag. I'm hungry, though. Maybe a seafood salad?"

"Sounds perfect."

Ellie and Malie continued to talk as I headed into the kitchen to assemble the salad. We'd stopped at a local farmers market, so not only did we have both shrimp and crab, we had giant avocados, fresh tomatoes, leafy lettuce, and locally made dressing as well. It warmed my heart to see Ellie smiling. I'm not sure what Malie said to her, but the light, which I feared might be permanently extinguished, was back in my best friend's eyes. We'd purchased a freshly baked baguette at the market that we'd never served, so I sliced it up and arranged it artfully on a plate with locally made cheese. I poured tea into a tall pitcher with ice and then brought everything out to the table on the patio, where we could dine with an unobstructed ocean view.

"Malie's work is so interesting." Ellie grinned. "She gets to work outdoors in this beautiful setting every day."

"Have you lived on the island your entire life?" I asked.

"Born and raised. As was my father and grandfather and his father before him."

"I love my mountain, but it really is beautiful here," I admitted. "So what exactly does your organization do?"

"Hawaii is home to a number of environmentally sensitive species, including humpback whales, monk seals, sea turtles, and dolphins. Our group participates in the health of our ecological system by educating people, monitoring endangered species, and organizing coastal cleanup projects, among other things. Most of our members are volunteers, and my job is to recruit and organize the volunteers for our area."

"Malie is having a small group meeting tomorrow. She invited me to attend," Ellie informed me. "I was hoping we could have the meeting here so I could keep Charlie company while you and the guys are at the luau."

"It's a small group of people, all residents and all very responsible," Malie assured me. "There will be between six and eight of us at the most. We'd planned to have the meeting at my apartment, but the view from this patio is much more inspiring."

"I don't see why that would be a problem," I answered. "I'd love to attend myself, but I promised Keoke I'd attend the luau, and he's been so great to us."

"Keoke is a generous sponsor of our organization," Malie informed me. "He gives not only of his time but of his money. We are very lucky to have his support. His cousin Pono is also a valued volunteer as well as my best friend. He will be attending the luau tomorrow and so will miss our meeting, but I promised to fill him in. Be sure to introduce yourself. Pono gets involved in the political side of what we do, so he has a tendency to lecture anyone who will listen, but under the gruff exterior is a man with a heart of gold."

"I understand that tomorrow's celebration is in honor of Pono's sister and her new fiancé," I said.

Malie frowned before answering. "Leia has become engaged to a developer who moved to the Islands a few years ago. I'm afraid that Pono and Anton don't really get along."

"Really? That must be difficult for Leia."

"I suppose."

I couldn't help but notice the guarded look that came across Malie's face.

"Personality conflict?" I prodded. I realize the issue of Anton and Pono's relationship was really none of my business, but you know me; I like to dig around in everyone's relationships. Perhaps that's because it keeps me from having time to look too closely into my own.

"Anton is a nice enough man, but he doesn't fully understand the fragile environment in which we live, or the long-range damage that can be inflicted if sensitive land is disturbed," Malie answered, although her comment seemed canned. "I understand that environmentalists and developers must learn to coexist, so I make every effort to provide education and guidance where I can, but Pono is more apt to fly off the handle and organize a sit-in or vandalize building sites if he believes our wildlife is being threatened. Pono and Anton have butted heads on more than one occasion, most recently when Pono convinced a judge to issue an injunction preventing Anton from breaking ground on the new resort he is trying to build on the south shore. Anton is appealing the decision, but for now, I guess it's causing him quite a large headache because he's taken on some pretty big investors who make a point of getting a return on their money."

"Is that the judge who's missing?" I asked.

"Actually, it is," Malie answered.

"There's a missing judge?" Ellie asked.

Between Malie and me, we filled Ellie in on the facts surrounding the strange disappearance of the judge's sailboat.

"I heard there were two other men with Judge Gregor at the time of his disappearance," I said.

"Yes, an environmental attorney by the name of Brian Boxer and a developer named Trenton Baldwin."

"Judge Gregor was sailing with a developer and an environmental attorney? Seems like an odd group," I commented.

"I know on the surface it seems that Judge Gregor must be a conservationist because he blocked Anton's project, but he's actually pretty neutral, as a judge should be. He tends to look at the specific project; he blocks some projects, while others he supports. In Anton's case, he wanted to build on a beach that is known as a favorite nesting place for hawksbill turtles. These turtles are considered to be an endangered species, so their nesting grounds are protected. Pono got the proof we needed and convinced the judge to issue the injunction."

"I bet Anton was mad," Ellie guessed.

"Mad does not even begin to describe the degree of his rage," Malie confirmed.

"I'm surprised Leia and Anton managed to stay together through all of that," I contributed.

Malie shrugged, but I could tell she wasn't as indifferent as she tried to appear. "They seem to love each other." Her face continued to be guarded. "I suppose that in the end love conquers all."

"So what are you working on now?" I asked as I refilled the iced tea glasses.

Malie smiled with genuine enthusiasm. "We are currently developing a script for a series of educational films we hope to make that we believe will educate locals and visitors alike about the proper care and treatment of our local turtle population. Every year countless turtles are injured or even killed due to the negligence of the people who share their environment. While a few of these incidences are vicious attacks on these beautiful animals, most often the individual or individuals responsible are simply ignorant of the degree to which their behavior affects these delicate creatures."

"Your project sounds fascinating," I said.

"You're welcome to join us if your schedule allows while you are visiting. During the development phase we try to meet once a week."

Ellie turned to me. "What time are the guys due back?"

"They didn't say for certain, but I'd guess any time now. I know they mentioned diving this afternoon. Do you dive?" I asked Malie.

"As often as I can make the time. Pono and I were diving a few months ago and found what looked to be debris from a shipwreck. There was nothing to verify which vessel the objects came from, but we thought it would be fun to try to locate the ship, so we began a structured search of the area. We still haven't found anything conclusive, but we've found enough to suggest something is there. We've been mapping our efforts, so we feel we are narrowing down the probable location of the ship itself, if there is indeed a ship to find."

"I'd love to dive on a sunken ship," I told her.

"We could use some extra divers. I should check with Pono, but if it's okay with him, maybe you and anyone else in your group who is certified can join us."

"Zak, Levi, and I are certified," I volunteered.

"Ellie?" Malie asked.

"I prefer to stay on the surface, but I like to snorkel. It would be fun to go along for the ride. Do you think the ship you're looking for contains some kind of treasure?" Ellie wondered.

"We really don't know. At this point, all we have are a few random items we found on the ocean floor and a sense of adventure that propels us to keep looking. The first thing we'll need to do is identify the wreck. If we can find something that is unique to a specific ship, such as an item with a name or family crest, or perhaps a unique piece of jewelry, we can go to the library to do some research to see what we're looking at. Once we know which vessel the artifacts we have recovered originated from, we can come up with a better plan. If the items turn out to be a major find, we will need additional equipment and financial backing. Personally, I'm not sure I want to get into something like that, but there are people we can turn the salvage operation over to if we get to that point."

"The local library would have this type of information?" Ellie asked.

"Not necessarily, but my uncle has an extensive library that has been handed down through the family for multiple generations. Within the library are very old documents such as ship manifests. I guess treasure hunting is in my blood; both my father and grandfather had the bug."

"Maybe you can have them help you with your search," I suggested.

"My father and grandfather are both dead. My uncle will be a valuable asset if we find something, but he never learned to dive. He's much more of an intellectual than an adventurer."

"Are there a lot of sunken ships in this area?" Ellie asked.

"Not as many as in the Bahamas, but we have our fair share of downed vessels."

I found myself hoping that Pono would agree to let us tag along. A treasure hunt for a sunken ship was exactly the type of distraction everyone in our battered group needed to take our minds off the problems we'd vowed to leave behind.

Later that evening, we decided to use one of the gift cards I'd won to treat ourselves to dinner in Kaanapali. Malie had recommended that we try one of the restaurants in the Whalers Village. Not only were there fantastic dining options but there were retail shops and a museum as well. Zak focused on the museum, Ellie preferred shopping, and Levi headed straight for the oceanfront bar at the Hula Grill.

I was torn. Either the bar or shopping sounded like a lot more fun than watching a movie about whales or looking at centuries' old artifacts, but Zak was my boyfriend and I felt that he deserved a little Zoe time.

"I think I'll go with Zak," I declared, like the wonderful girlfriend I am.

"Should we meet for dinner in an hour?" Ellie asked.

"Sounds good."

I slipped my hand into Zak's as we headed up the stairs to the museum, though I couldn't help but notice the tops in the window of the shop Ellie was heading into.

"This is nice." I leaned my head against Zak's arm as we found a seat in the back. The tiny movie theater was empty at this time of day.

"Are you sure you wouldn't rather be shopping with Ellie?"

Yes, I would.

"Are you kidding?" I answered. "I love whales. Besides, I missed you today. It seems like we haven't had a lot of time together lately."

"Yeah." Zak sighed. "Things have been hectic."

"I'm looking forward to the luau tomorrow, but it would be nice to have some alone time too."

Zak put his arm around me and pulled me close to his body. I could hear his heart beating against my ear. I've discovered that the steady rhythm of Zak's heart has the ability to calm me even when it feels like the world is spinning out of control.

"I've been to the museum before if you'd like to do something else," Zak offered.

"Did you have something in mind?"

"We don't have to meet the others for an hour. We could take a walk down the beach, or maybe look through a couple of shops."

"You hate shopping."

"Yes, but I love you." Zak kissed me gently.

Suddenly, I wished we could head back to the house, but we only had one car and Levi and Ellie had planned a full evening of entertainment.

"Besides," Zak added, "there's one store I'd like to check out. You game?"

"Of course."

Zak left a large donation for the museum and we left while the movie was still playing. We walked hand in hand through the village, which featured a variety of shops catering to a wide range of tastes and interests. When Zak walked into a jewelry shop, I almost had a coronary. It was possible he might be in need of a new watch, but I feared he was looking for something of a more personal nature. I knew Zak wanted to take our relationship to the next level, but to be honest, the next level really wasn't something I was quite ready for.

"I saw this the last time I was here." Zak picked up a gold necklace with a delicate chain and an artfully crafted sea turtle. "It made me think of you. Do you like it?"

I frowned. "The last time you were here? When was that?"

We'd only been dating for six months, and Zak had only been back in Ashton Falls for eight.

"A couple of years ago. When we walked by the window, I realized they had the same necklace."

"You saw the necklace and it made you think of me a couple of years ago? You weren't even living in Ashton Falls then."

Zak placed the necklace around my neck and latched the clasp. It really was beautiful. "Just because I wasn't living in Ashton Falls doesn't mean I wasn't thinking of you."

I would never admit it, but I didn't think about Zak much at all during the years he was traveling the world.

"You used to think of me after you left Ashton Falls? Why?"

The truth of the matter was that we had been arch nemeses before we'd reunited the previous fall.

"Why do you think?" Zak asked.

"You didn't even like me," I pointed out.

"Of course I liked you. I loved you. Always have and always will."

I was pretty sure I was going to cry.

"Always?" I whispered.

Chapter 4

Saturday June 28

"I can't believe how beautiful this is," I gasped as Zak helped me from the seaplane that had pulled up to the dock of the private island where Keoke's grandparents lived. There were several smaller homes near the dock that I imagined must belong to the workers, while the main plantation house was set on the far side of the island to take advantage of the spectacular views.

"Keoke's family has owned the island for several generations and they take great pride in the home they've created. Wait until you see the house. You're going to love the simplicity of the plantation style combined with the elegance and beauty of the natural wood and bamboo."

The path leading from the dock to the house was heavily planted with plumeria, hibiscus, orchids, roses, and other fragrant plants. Exotic birds greeted visitors with song as artful waterfalls cascaded into pools of clear water. No expense had been spared to create the perfect tropical paradise. As we neared the house, the path, which felt like something created for a Disney ride, opened up onto a large lawn with strategically planted shade trees. In the center was a big pond where birds of a variety of breeds floated on the clear, fresh water.

The single-story house was spread out over the flat landscape beyond a pool and deck area and, as Zak had promised, it was spectacular. He hadn't mentioned the size of the estate, but I was willing to bet that the square footage rivaled Zak's home at least.

"Look at the view." I sighed.

"And the outdoor kitchen," Zak added.

"And the girls." Levi drooled as his eyes lit up at the sight of dozens of beautiful women gathered in small groups around the elaborate deck.

"Remember, we're at an engagement party, so be careful who you canoodle with," I warned.

"Don't worry; I'll stay away from the bride-to-be, but everyone else is fair game."

I laughed. It was good to see Levi back to his old self.

"Is that where they're cooking the pig?" I nodded toward an area set well away from the gathering, where smoke was curling its way into the air. The BBQ pit had been placed behind a wall of shrubbery so as not to disturb the peaceful landscape.

"Looks like," Zak said. "We should find Keoke to let him know we're here."

"You guys go ahead. I'll catch up with you later." Levi headed toward a group of women who were sitting near the pool, sipping brightly colored drinks.

Zak wound his fingers through mine as we continued toward the house. There were a lot more people attending the party than I'd initially thought there would be. I wondered why Malie wasn't attending as well, since she knew Keoke and was familiar with the island and so must have visited in the past. There was a stage set up at the edge of the grassy area. Zak had mentioned that there would be entertainment. I couldn't wait to watch the fire twirlers. I'd seen a demonstration on television and it had totally amazed me that the men who participated never got burned. If it were me twirling fire batons, it would be safe to bet that I'd have the entire island engulfed in a firestorm in a matter of minutes. In addition to the fire twirlers, Zak had promised hula dancers, knife throwers, and Polynesian drummers.

"Zachary." An elderly Hawaiian woman who had to be in her late eighties greeted us as we walked through the front door and into the cool interior of the house. "Where have you been, child?"

"Tutu, how are you?" Zak hugged the old woman.

"What has it been, a year? Two?" the woman scolded.

"I'm not traveling as much as I used to," Zak explained. "I've decided it might be time to settle down and stay in one place for a while."

The woman looked at me.

"This is Zoe Donovan. Zoe, this is Tutu, Keoke's grandmother."

"I'm glad to meet you." I extended my hand but was quickly wrapped in a hug. I found the woman was surprisingly strong for her age.

"Aren't you a pretty little thing?" Tutu commented after taking a step back and looking me up and down.

Normally, I hate it when people make reference to my diminutive size, but coming from this lovely woman, I could only smile at the compliment.

Tutu turned to Zak. "I can see why you've been staying close to home. She's lovely. I hope I'll be invited to the wedding."

"Oh, there's no wedding," I said. "We're just dating."

The woman smiled in such a way as to suggest that she knew things about me even I didn't know before leading us farther into the interior of the house.

"Is Keoke around?" Zak asked.

"He was here a minute ago," Tutu answered. "I think he might have gone to check on the pig. If he isn't there, you can most likely find him in the kitchen. He takes the food for these shindigs very seriously."

"Leia and Anton?" Zak inquired about the bride-and groom-to-be.

"I haven't seen either of them all day. I'm sure they want to make a grand entrance. You know Leia; she's had a flare for the dramatic ever since she was a little girl."

"I guess we'll go and find Keoke then," Zak said. He kissed Tutu on the cheek. "Save me a dance?"

"Count on it."

"She seems nice," I commented as we left the house by the side door and headed down the path to the BBQ pit.

"She *is* nice. Very nice. I didn't realize how much I missed her until I saw her standing in the entry. I really do need to make an effort to get back here more often." Zak turned to me and kissed me lightly on the lips. "*We* need to get back here more often," he clarified.

"I'd like that. It really is beautiful here, and the people are so nice. Did I tell you that Ellie and I met a woman by the name of Malie yesterday? She's involved in the rescue and preservation of the animals in the area, much as I am in Ashton Falls. She really hit it off with Ellie, which is why she decided to opt out this evening. Her organization is having a planning meeting of some type tonight."

"Malie is a friend of the family."

"Which made me wonder why she isn't here."

Zak stopped walking and turned to face the ocean. We had come to a slight rise that afforded us a spectacular view. "I haven't been here for a couple of years, so I only know what I do via hearsay, but it seems Malie dated Anton before he started seeing Leia."

"She didn't mention that," I said.

"When Anton first came to Maui, Malie was involved in a movement to block a business complex he wanted to build. In the course of arguing the opposite sides of the issue, they got to know each other and started dating. I think it was pretty serious for a while. Anton and Pono didn't get along, and since Pono is Malie's best friend, that caused a certain amount of tension in their relationship, but from what I heard, things were moving along until Malie brought Anton to a party here on the island and he met Leia. From what I understand, it was love at first sight between the two. Anton broke things off with Malie, who was crushed. Even though Pono never approved of Anton and Malie's relationship, he was outraged that his sister stole his best friend's guy. I guess it colored his judgment, and not only did he effectively disown his sister but he began to aggressively challenge Anton over every project he became involved in."

"So why is he here today?"

"Tutu and other family members convinced him to attend. Leia is his sister, and the family has always been very close. The general feeling is that it would be destructive to the family as a whole to let something like this come between the two of them. Pono is a good guy, so he agreed to attend, but based on what Keoke has told me, he isn't thrilled to be here."

"Wow, that's really too bad."

"Yeah. It is unfortunate, although Keoke tells me that Anton and Leia really love each other, and he believes everything will work out in the long run. Malie has forgiven Anton and Leia, so I'm sure she can convince Pono to as well."

"I never did have a chance to tell you about the treasure hunt Malie invited us to participate in if Pono agrees."

"Treasure hunt?" Zak looked intrigued.

I explained about the relics Malie and Pono had found and the wreck they hoped to find.

"A treasure hunt is every diver's dream," Zak said. "Maybe we should find Pono and talk to him about it."

"Any idea where to look? I asked.

"Let's ask Keoke if he's seen him."

"So about this pig . . ." I changed the subject back to the wonderful smell emitting from the pit. "They roast the whole thing?"

"Head and all," Zak verified.

I felt my stomach roll.

"Don't worry; there's plenty of other food if you don't want to eat the pig, although it is delicious."

"Yeah, well . . ." I hesitated. "We'll see."

The trail wound its way from the house along an incline to the flat expanse where the pit had been dug. While the pit was isolated from the lawn side by high shrubs, it was open to the water on the ocean side. Keoke was sitting on a rock wall overlooking the ocean. Most of the guests were in the house or on the deck near the pool, so Keoke was alone with his BBQ masterpiece.

"You made it." Keoke grinned. He hugged both Zak and me.

Keoke is a large man with a commanding presence and a genuine smile. He was dressed as if he were preparing to enter a boardroom rather than entertain guests at a luau. I had the feeling that the man was a workaholic who didn't know how to relax. The only concession to his immaculate presentation was a small tattoo on the inside of his wrist.

"You're here alone?" Zak asked.

"I needed some quiet time. It's been a hectic and stressful couple of days." Keoke gazed out over the horizon. He looked like a man with serious things on his mind. I had to wonder what had caused the worry lines around eyes that appeared not to have seen a full night's sleep for quite some time.

"I can imagine," Zak said. I was pretty sure Zak was referring to the stress caused by planning the party, but I was pretty sure there was more going on than met the eye.

"Your home is lovely," I offered.

"It's actually my grandparents' home, but I love it here."

"You live on Oahu?" I asked.

He nodded. "My business is there, but I come out here whenever I can get away."

"We're really enjoying your home on Maui. The house is spectacular and the view . . . let's just say it has to be one of the best on the island. We're having a fantastic time and I want to thank you again for letting us use it."

"I'm happy to have the whole gang," Keoke assured me. "Although I was sorry to hear that things didn't work out with your friend. Breakups can be tough."

"Yes," I acknowledged, "they can, but Ellie seems to be doing better. She's doing things to take her mind off her problems. She even made a new friend on the island. I think you know her: Malie."

"Malie and I are good friends. She is a wonderful person with a genuine heart. Your friend will do well in her care. I'm guessing she has her involved in some project already."

"She does," I informed him. "How did you know?"

"That's Malie's way. She adopts strays and finds things for them to do that will keep them busy and give them a sense of belonging and purpose. She really is an exceptional person."

"She mentioned that she was also friends with your cousin Pono. I hope to meet him while I'm here."

Keoke frowned. "I'm not sure where Pono got off to. I'm afraid he got into an argument with Anton early this morning before anyone else arrived and both of them stormed off. I haven't seen either since. My guess is that they left the island, although I'm not supposed to tell anyone that until we can verify it. Poor Leia is beside herself with worry. She insists that Anton wouldn't just take off on such an important day, but we've looked everywhere. I hoped the men would return before the party got underway, but it looks like they'll both be no-shows."

"It's a shame Leia will have to attend her own engagement party alone."

"I knew it was a bad idea for the elders to insist that Pono attend." Keoke ran a hand through his black hair. "There is too much tension between the two men, and Leia is stuck in the middle of their battle. It's hard when your fiancé and brother basically hate each other."

"Malie told me about the injunction."

"That is just one of many conflicts," Keoke said. "If Pono shows up, I'll tell him you were looking for him."

"If I don't meet him today, I'm sure I will tomorrow. Malie invited us to go diving with her and Pono," I informed our host.

"That will be fun," Keoke promised. "I'd come along myself, but I really need to get back to Oahu. Maybe we can get together another time."

"I'd like that."

"There's a path that leads down the hill and into the jungle. I would recommend it as an ideal path for young lovers," Keoke suggested. "It winds through beautiful flowers and ends at a cascading waterfall that flows into a freshwater pond. I doubt the others will bother to make the hike, so it should be deserted as well."

Zak looked at me. "You game for a hike?"

"It sounds perfect."

"Before we go, is there anything we can do to help you?" I asked Keoke. "Anything other than uncover that pig, I mean?"

Keoke laughed. "Go ahead and take your walk. I imagine the festivities will begin at sunset, which will give you a couple of hours to enjoy some time alone."

Zak and I set off. It was warm but not hot, and the narrow path through dense foliage was deserted, lending an air of tropical isolation to the journey. It would have been easy to imagine we were all alone on a deserted island if not for the faint sound of music in the distance.

"What exactly does Keoke do for a living?" I asked.

"He's a real estate investor."

"So he buys houses and stuff?"

"More like commercial property. He's involved in both purchasing existing property as well as investing in new development."

"Has he ever invested with Anton?"

Zak shrugged. "I'm not sure. We don't talk specifics when we get together."

"How did you meet him?"

"Years ago, after I started my business, he asked me to bid on a software program for a security system that was going to be included in a high-rise on Oahu. I got the job and we became friends."

The path wound through the foliage and toward a sheer cliff overlooking waves crashing onto the rocks below. The water hit the rock wall with such force that it sprayed moisture onto the path.

"Wouldn't want to fall from here," I commented as I navigated the slippery walkway.

"That wouldn't be fun at all," Zak agreed. "Maybe we can go for a swim when we get to the pond."

"Sounds nice. It's such a fantastic day. Not too hot, not too cold."

"Every day in Hawaii is spectacular. I was here during a tropical storm that was pretty gnarly, though. I'd never seen waves that high before in my life."

"I'd love to see the really big waves." I stepped over a narrow gully that had been washed away by a hard rain with heavy runoff.

"We'll come back in the winter. The waves on the north shore of Oahu are something else. Not as big as the ones I saw during the storm, but awesome all the same."

I stopped walking. "What's that sound?"

Zak listened. "I'm guessing we've disturbed a wild boar."

"They have wild pigs here?"

"Yeah, quite a few. They can be dangerous, so if we happen to come across one, don't approach it."

By the time we got to the waterfall and the pool beneath it, I was hot and sticky. The Islands were a lot more humid than I was used to. The feel of the water in the crystal-clear pool as it caressed my naked body was probably the most sensual thing I'd ever experienced. Zak and I laughed and played in the waterfall as we swam beneath its gentle flow. After we swam, we laid on a rock to dry off and then dressed and headed back through the jungle toward the house.

"Those cave paintings on the wall behind the falls were really interesting," I commented as we walked through the tropical jungle.

"Yeah," Zak agreed as he swatted at a bug that had landed on his arm. "They looked old. I know a native tribe lived on Maui long before it was inhabited by Europeans."

"Malie mentioned that the island is the source of several fables, including a very romantic tale of an English sailor who became shipwrecked on the island and a beautiful Hawaiian princess."

"I've heard that one, and while it's sweet and romantic, it doesn't end well," Zak warned me.

"Don't tell me. Malie said something similar, and Ellie and I decided we'd rather imagine that the couple lived happily ever after and had many children and grandchildren to comfort them in their old age."

Zak laughed.

Malie had hinted that the tale was actually quite tragic, but I for one didn't want to dwell on tragedy at this particular moment.

"I can hear the drummers," Zak said as we neared the house.

"I hope Anton and Pono have shown up. I can't imagine what Leia must be going through. To let something like this happen on the day of her engagement party makes me think less of both men."

We'd almost reached the main part of the property when we saw the large group gathered on the lawn, watching as drummers beat a rhythm for dancers who moved in tune to the music. There were several men stationed at the pit the pig was being roasted in. Zak and I came up to it from behind.

"It's time to uncover our meal," Keoke announced. "I need to go to make a speech, but feel free to stay and watch, if you'd like."

I was about to decline when Zak announced that he'd like to watch.

Several men began the process of removing the layers covering the pig. Once the dirt was swept away, the tarp that had covered the whole pit was removed. Several rocks were set aside before the burlap that had covered the object wrapped in chicken wire and seaweed was removed. The pig was lifted out and set on a table, where the chicken wire was cut open. As the seaweed was peeled away, I heard one of the men gasp. I'd already decided I wasn't going to look at the eerie sight of the roasted beast, but for some reason I found that I couldn't quite quell my curiosity. I inched toward the edge of the table and took a peek. What I saw caused the small amount of food I'd nibbled to work its way up toward my throat.

"It can't be that bad," Zak teased as I stood with my hand over my mouth, struggling not to vomit.

"Oh my God," a man standing next to me uttered.

Zak frowned and walked toward the table and glanced at the charred flesh. "Get Keoke," he told one of the men.

He covered the body and returned to my side. "I think you should wait with the others." He took my hand and led me down the path to the lawn, where the rest of the guests were waiting. After locating Levi, he handed me off before returning to the pit with Keoke and a few others.

"What's going on?" Levi asked.

"The body in the pit wasn't a pig."

Chapter 5

Sunday, June 29

When I'd agreed to call Tiffany at nine o'clock in the morning, I'd failed to take into account the time difference. She was going into work on her day off because she'd sensed my discomfort at not having anyone there with everything that was going on, so I felt I needed to get up early to make the call. The problem was that there wasn't enough caffeine on the planet to wake me up after the long night I'd had.

The body in the pit had been Anton's. No one knew exactly how he came to be there. Keoke had personally overseen the burial of the pig, although he hadn't stayed in attendance once it had been left to cook. Keoke said he and Pono had gotten up early to get the pig prepped for the day-long roasting. They'd covered the pit at around eight and Keoke had returned to the house to do some work before the guests began to arrive. He reported that he'd remained in his grandfather's office most of the morning but had heard Pono and Anton arguing on the lawn from an open window. He hadn't seen either of the men after that and had no idea what it was they were arguing about.

The only people on the island prior to the arrival of the first boat filled with guests at two o'clock had been Keoke and his grandparents; Anton and Leia; Anton's best man, Jeffrey Highlander, who Keoke hadn't met prior to that morning; Leia's best friend and maid of honor Cora Bell, who Keoke had known for years; Pono; the household staff and plantation workers; and four men from the catering company who'd arrived early to set up. Additionally, the florist and her assistant had stopped by but left after dropping off the flowers.

The police didn't want anyone to leave until everyone had been interviewed, so it was well into the early morning by the time Zak, Levi, and I returned to the house on Maui.

The last I heard, they still hadn't located Pono, but that was hours ago, so there might very well be a reasonable solution to this horrible murder by this point.

Zak, Levi, and Ellie were still sleeping soundly, so I made coffee and took it out onto the deck. Charlie sniffed around on the beach while I sipped the dark brew and willed my brain to work. It was light, but the beach was still deserted. The only sign of life I saw other than a boat in the distance was a school of spinner dolphins out for a morning swim. It was peaceful and relaxing to watch their antics, but deep in my gut I knew that this trip, which had started off so peacefully, had suddenly become much more complicated.

I knew that Anton's death wasn't my business. I'd never even met the man, but I'd seen the depth of despair in Leia's eyes and the realization of his cousin Pono's probable detainment on Keoke's face. I'd promised myself and everyone else that I absolutely, positively would not get involved, but everyone knew that my promise was more likely than not empty.

"Hey, Tiff." I was yawning when she picked up.

"I'm surprised you called. When I suggested nine o'clock, I forgot about the time difference."

"No worries. I was awake," I lied.

"How was the luau?"

"It was . . ." I paused to look for a word that could sum up the events of the previous day. "Eventful."

"So tell me all about it. Was the island beautiful?"

"It was exceptional. I even got to swim under a waterfall."

"Wow, I'm jealous. How was the pig?"

"Missing, actually."

"Missing?"

I decided to fill Tiffany in on the less pleasant events of the day.

"The dead guy was in the pit where the pig should have been?" Tiffany said. "How could that have happened?"

"I don't know. People were around most of the day, although Keoke did say that he hadn't stayed to guard the pit once the pig had been buried, and there were only a handful of people on the island during the morning hours. The pit was set back from the house and shielded by large shrubs, so it's reasonable that someone could have made the switch and not been seen, especially if they had help lifting the pig out and putting the man into the hole. I guess the whole thing was a fairly complicated process, so the person who made the switch must have had help."

"That's just so wrong. His poor fiancée."

"Yeah, she was kind of a mess."

"Well, I should think so. Was the man dead before he was baked?" Tiffany asked.

"I don't have lot of information, but I did get a pretty good look and there was a knife in the man's back. Hopefully, he was long dead before he was lowered into the hole in the ground."

"He was facedown in the pit?" Tiffany asked.

"Yes, thank God."

"Are there any suspects?"

"At this point the prime one is the bride-to-be's brother."

"Oh no. That poor woman. If I'd uncovered a pit and expected to find a pig but found a man instead, I wouldn't be able to sleep for weeks."

"Yeah, it was pretty bad. I talked to Salinger." I decided to change the subject. There wasn't anything I could do to help Anton, Leia, Pono, or Keoke at the moment, and the image of the dead man in the pit was already engraved in my brain. Talking about it was making it ten times worse.

"Did he have any insight on the dead animals?" Tiffany asked.

"No, but he promised to look into it."

"Do you think he will?"

I yawned again. "Probably not. Did the dogs from Bryton Lake show up?"

"They arrived yesterday afternoon. Scott came over to give them all full exams. He said they seemed fine but agreed that we should keep them isolated for a few days."

"Speaking of Scott, did you ever ask him out?" Tiffany had confessed to having a thing for our local vet and I'd recommended that she ask him out. She'd agreed to do it, although I suspected she hadn't.

"Not yet," Tiffany admitted. "Asking a guy out is hard."

"And you don't think guys feel the same way?" I asked.

"You think they *do*?"

"Sure, if they really like the girl they're asking. My feeling is that he'll say yes, but even if he doesn't, at least you'll know where he stands."

"I know you're right. I'll do it before you get back."

"Good."

"I called your mom yesterday to warn her to keep her dogs in. She said she ran into one of the women she knew from her birthing class who told her that her cat died for no apparent reason a few weeks ago. It could be an unrelated incident, but with the other dead animals, I thought I should mention it."

"Did my mom give you a name?"

"No, she didn't say."

"Maybe I'll call her later to see what I can find out. With everything that's going on, it's probably a good idea to follow every lead."

"You're going to be busy if you're going to investigate the strange happenings here, solve a murder in Hawaii, and make sure all your friends are happy and having a good time."

A truer thing had never been said.

By the time the rest of the gang had emerged from their rooms, we'd been notified by Malie that Pono had been taken to the station for questioning. According to Malie, who'd come over at Ellie's insistence, Pono had gone sailing alone after arguing with Anton. He'd borrowed a boat on the island but decided not to return to the party, so he'd rented a slip for the night in the marina near his home. He'd run into a friend at the marina and the two had gone out drinking. Pono stated that he hadn't gotten back to his apartment until well after midnight. The problem was that Anton had to have been put into the pit between eight a.m. and noon, and Pono hadn't arrived at the marina until after four. He could easily have killed Anton and then sailed away before anyone knew he was missing.

Zak called and talked to Keoke, who reported that Pono insisted he was innocent. The police didn't have any physical evidence to keep him so would most likely let him go before the end of the day. Other than Pono, there were no other immediate suspects. Anton was a businessman who'd made enemies along the way, but it was determined that whoever put Anton in the fire pit had to have been on the island before the main group of guests arrived. The police had interviewed everyone, but no one stood out as a suspect.

"I can't believe this has happened." Malie looked shell-shocked.

"I hate to bring up a delicate subject, but I understand that you dated Anton before Leia became involved with him," I said.

"Yes, we dated," Malie admitted, "and yes, I was hurt when he chose Leia. It's the reason I didn't go to the luau."

"I'm sorry," I offered. "I'm sure this must be hard for you."

Malie nodded her head as she wiped away a tear.

"It seems you knew Anton pretty well. Can you think of anyone who would want to hurt him?" I asked.

Malie looked at me. "Why do you want to know? Are you working with the police?"

"Absolutely not." I looked directly at Zak, who simply rolled his eyes. "I'm just curious."

"Zoe is sort of an amateur sleuth," Ellie explained. "She doesn't mean to be, but somehow she seems to get caught up in things any time there's a murder at home. She's really very good."

"She might be able to help clear Pono," Levi added. "If he's innocent, that is."

"You don't think he's innocent?" Malie asked.

Levi shrugged. "How would I know? I've never even met the guy, but in my experience, if he walks like a killer and talks like a killer . . ."

"If Malie says Pono is innocent, he is." Ellie stuck up for her new friend.

"I've run into Pono a few times when I've visited, and I have to say I agree with Malie," Zak added.

"Then we need to talk to Pono," I said. "Maybe we can invite him to come over once the police are done with him."

"I'll leave him a message," Malie agreed. "I know it looks like he's guilty, but I promise you that Pono would never hurt Anton. While it's true he didn't like the man, Pono would never hurt anyone, and he definitely would never do anything to cause this degree of pain to his sister."

"I believe you," I offered. "One thing I've discovered along the way is that the person who appears to be the most likely killer rarely is. I'm not sure how we can help, but I promise you we'll try. In the meantime, I'm starving. Is there a place to get a really big breakfast around here? We never did have dinner last night."

"There are several good places in Lahaina," Malie said. "My favorite is Makani's. My good friend Luana owns it with her husband, Palani. You might have met him. He catered the luau."

"So he would have been on the island early yesterday, before the other guests arrived, in order to set up?"

"Yes, he went over in the morning along with several helpers. Do you think he might have seen something?"

"Perhaps. Why did Keoke hire a caterer from Maui if the party was closer to Oahu?" I asked.

"Honestly, I'm not sure," Malie answered. "When I first heard that Palani was catering the affair, I thought it odd on several different levels."

"How so?" I asked.

"I think I'll let him explain things to you himself."

Chapter 6

Lahaina is a popular tourist town. The main thoroughfare is lined on both sides with inviting shops selling everything from fine art to Hawaiian-themed mugs and T-shirts. We parked two blocks from the main street and walked to our destination on crowded sidewalks past colorful displays of local wares that gave the area a festive feel. I noticed several shops I really wanted to check out after we'd had our meal.

One of the gift cards I'd won thanks to my display of public humiliation was for a clothing store that carried everything from bikinis to sundresses. I couldn't help but pause in front as we passed a display of colorful sandals. There were several pairs of neon flip-flops I was certain I really needed to have.

"Yellow or orange?" I asked Zak.

He paused to consider the selection. "Personally, I like the neon blue."

"Really?" I scrunched up my nose. "I was leaning toward the yellow."

"The yellow is nice." Zak smiled.

"I see what you did there," I said once I realized that Zak had totally manipulated me into choosing between the yellow and orange by suggesting a color he knew I wouldn't like.

He merely put his arm around my shoulder and followed me into the store, where I ended up spending double the value on my gift card.

Did I mention that the shopping in Lahaina is to die for?

"So what's next?" Zak asked as I emerged with my packages.

"Breakfast," Levi said firmly.

I wanted to buy souvenirs for my dad and mom and Harper, but that could wait until after we ate. I had a feeling finding the perfect gifts might take a while. Dad was easy because he'd appreciate anything I bought, and there were lots of stores selling adorable outfits for babies, but I had no idea what to get for my mom. Somehow I didn't think a Hawaiian print shirt or a pair of turtle earrings were going to make all that much of an impression on a woman who had traveled the world and shopped in the most exclusive stores everywhere she went.

Lahaina not only provides a wide range of shopping opportunities but a smorgasbord of restaurants as well. Makani's was a popular place right on the waterfront. We were shown to a table on the outdoor deck overlooking the ocean. The food choices were varied and included traditional Hawaiian offerings as well as the common breakfast items found at any restaurant on the mainland. Zak and Levi ordered a breakfast that included eggs, spam, sticky rice, and gravy, while Ellie and I decided to try the macadamia nut waffles. Malie opted for a fish and rice dish featuring local fish caught just that morning.

"What a beautiful spot to have breakfast," Ellie commented as Luana poured us each a glass of fresh-squeezed papaya juice.

"We were very lucky to get this location for our restaurant," Luana said.

"Zak and Zoe were at Keoke's luau yesterday," Malie informed her friend. "They hoped to have a word with Palani because he was on the island as well."

"Did you know Anton?" Luana asked us.

"No," Zak answered. "Keoke and I are friends and I know the family, but it's been a few years since I've visited, so I never did have the pleasure of meeting Leia's fiancé."

"Not to speak ill of the dead, but you didn't miss much by not meeting that snake."

"You didn't get along?" Zak asked.

"Anton wanted to buy this whole block of buildings. He had plans to build an oceanfront resort. There are six business owners in all. He'd managed to convince three to sell, but the rest of us have been holding out. It's been a nasty battle, hanging on to what is ours, since the three who have signed contracts were beginning to put pressure on those of us who don't care about the money he was offering."

"Was he offering a fair price?" I asked.

"More than fair. The three who signed contracts got double what their businesses were worth. As for us, we love our restaurant. Opening it has been our dream since Palani and I first met. We worked hard to make this a reality and have no wish to sell at any price."

"I guess that put you in a tough spot," Ellie sympathized.

"It did. The contracts the businesses signed were contingent on all six owners selling. If even one refused to sell, no one would get the money Anton was offering. Right now, we are not alone in our decision not to sell, but Palani was afraid that the other two business owners would give in. If they did, we would have little choice but to sell. I shouldn't say it, but when we found out that the body in the pit was Anton's, we actually felt relief. Maybe without him in the picture we can convince the others to hold out."

"I wonder who'll take over Anton's business now," I mused.

"Anton owned a large corporation with many employees," Luana answered. "I know he had a partner as well, although I believe he works out of an office on the mainland. Still, I suppose they had a plan for such an event. I only hope whoever takes over the decision making for Maui is more reasonable than Anton."

Luana stopped talking and looked toward a group that had just walked into the restaurant. "It looks like I have a new party to seat. I'll send Palani out when he has a chance."

"You don't think . . . ?" I asked after Luana walked away.

"I'm sure Palani had nothing to do with Anton's death," Malie assured us. "Although I agree that he was an odd choice for Keoke to make when he hired someone to provide food for the event. For one thing, Keoke's grandparents have a cook who lives on the island. A very good cook. It would have been easier and less expensive for him only to hire kitchen helpers. And then there is the matter of proximity. Keoke had to cart Palani and his helpers, and all of the food and supplies that were needed, a fairly long distance by seaplane. It would have made much more sense to hire a company out of Oahu if the cook couldn't handle it."

"You're right; Keoke's choice of caterer does seem odd. Does Keoke know of the battle between Palani and Anton?" I asked.

"He does, which is another reason why asking Palani to cater Anton's engagement party made no sense."

"Do you think Palani's presence on the island was orchestrated specifically so he could kill Anton? Maybe Palani bribed Keoke or threatened him in some way to get the job."

"No," Malie said. "I realize how it sounds, but Palani is a good guy. He'd never hurt Anton."

"What about the others who went along to help?" Ellie asked. "If Luana and Palani are forced to sell, their employees would lose their jobs."

"I don't know who Palani brought with him yesterday, but I guess it couldn't hurt to ask," Malie answered. "Though killing a man seems like a lot of trouble to go to just to keep a job."

"True, unless the killer had another motive as well," I added.

We stopped talking when a waitress brought our food. Not only did everything look delicious but the servings were generous enough to share. Or at least I *thought* they were. In the end, the golden waffles with homemade macadamia butter and warm syrup were so yummy, I ended up eating the entire plateful. At least we probably weren't going to go diving today as planned.

The conversation drifted away from murder toward the long list of possible pastimes we might pursue while on the island. Ellie hoped to visit Hana, while Zak and Levi couldn't wait to try out the surfboards in the storage room. Malie recommended watching the sunrise from Haleakala, while I was totally focused on the treasure hunt that, by necessity, had been delayed.

Palani came out to join us just as we were finishing our meal. He was tall and thin, with a nice smile and a boyish charm.

"How was your food?" he asked.

"So good." I rubbed my stomach.

"Luana said you had questions about the luau yesterday."

"If you have a few minutes," I said.

Palani smiled at Malie. "Any friends of Malie are friends of mine. What would you like to know?"

"What time did you arrive at the island yesterday?" I asked.

"My crew and I arrived around seven-thirty."

"And who did you bring with you?"

"Four of my employees: Darwin, Larry, Stephanie, and Alfonso."

"Did any of them know Anton?"

Palani paused. "They all know *of* him due to the project he is working on, but as far as I know, none of the four are personal friends of his. Of course, I don't really know all that much about the personal lives of my employees, so who knows?"

"But you hadn't seen any of the four speaking to Anton?"

"No, I hadn't."

"And who else was on the island at that time?" I asked.

Palani frowned. "You seem to have a lot of questions. Are you working with the police?"

"No," I answered. "My friends and I are just trying to help figure out what might have happened. It seems Pono is the only suspect at this point. It will help his case if we can give the police someone else to look at."

"Keoke and Pono were at the pit tending to the pig when I arrived," Palani said. "Keoke's grandmother was in the garden picking flowers for an arrangement she was working on, and his grandfather was watching television in the study. I know Leia and Anton were there, as well as their friends, Jeffrey and Cora. I never did run into Anton or Leia. I assumed they were getting ready for the big day. Jeffrey and Cora joined the guests in the yard once they began to arrive at around two, but I don't know where they were prior to that."

"Keoke mentioned household staff?"

"There is a live-in housekeeper as well as a gardener and a cook on the estate. I believe all three were on-site, although the only staff I spoke to was the cook. Her name is Gretchen. She has been with the family for a long time and wanted to keep an eye on her kitchen while my people and I were preparing the feast Keoke ordered."

"Please don't take this the wrong way," I began. "The food you prepared is some of the best I've ever had, but why did Keoke hire you to cater the party if his grandparents have their own cook?"

Palani looked surprised by the question. "I'm not sure. Keoke approached me about the job several weeks ago. We discussed a menu and other specifics, such as the time commitment and transportation to and from the island. Luana and I do well, but there is little profit margin in a restaurant such as ours, so when I heard the price Keoke was offering for a day's work, I jumped at it. I didn't really stop to wonder why he would ask me to provide the food rather than having his grandparents' cook do it."

"Do you think Gretchen was capable of handling such a large party?"

Palani shrugged. "Keoke's grandparents have parties all the time. Perhaps Keoke wanted her to have a day off to enjoy the festivities, although she didn't seem very happy to be left out of the food preparation."

"Is there anyone you can think of who might want Anton dead?" I wondered.

"Besides me and Pono? Yes. The man wasn't popular. There are a lot of people who will rejoice at his passing." Palani looked at Malie. "I'm sorry, Mal. I know how you felt about him, but you know what I say is true."

"It's okay. I understand," Malie said, although she looked sad all the same.

Palani looked back at me and continued. "If what you're really asking is whether there was someone on the island during the morning hours who would want him dead, then the answer is, other than Pono and me, not really. I promise you, however, that I didn't do it. Now, I really should get back to the kitchen."

"Thank you for speaking to us," I offered.

After Palani walked away, I looked at the other people sitting with me at the table. "Well?"

"This is not going to be an easy murder to solve," Malie guessed.

"Probably not," I agreed. "Do we continue to try?"

I looked around the table. I don't think any of us had planned to use our vacation to track down the killer of a man we'd never even met. I felt bad for Malie, who *did* know him, and for Pono, even though I'd yet to meet him. Keoke had been so nice to us that part of me really wanted to help him figure out what had happened the morning of the luau. But I also wanted to go diving and try surfing and spend a day reading next to the pool.

"Let's talk to Pono and then decide," Levi said.

After breakfast, Zak suggested that we take a walk to the edge of town, where Lahaina's famous banyan tree was located. The 137-year-old tree towers over almost an acre and is said to be the largest such tree in the United States. Thanks to its aerial roots, which grow into trunks when they touch the ground, the shady tree is now supported by at least sixteen trunks in addition to the original.

"The shade from this tree feels like a slice of heaven." I sighed.

I love Hawaii, but I had to admit that after living in Ashton Falls my entire life, I was having a hard time getting used to the heat and humidity.

"We should check out the old courthouse," Zak said.

I could tell that Levi and Ellie were as bored as I was by the suggestion, but Malie's eyes lit up like a Christmas tree at Zak's suggestion.

"The courthouse houses the only U.S. flag to have flown over a kingdom, a republic, a territory, and a state," Malie shared.

I'm a bit embarrassed to say I mostly tuned out as Malie explained that the flag was designed in 1812, during the reign of King Kamehameha I. She told us that the eight red, blue, and white stripes represent the eight major islands of Hawaii, while the canton consists of the British Union Jack, representing Hawaii's original ties with Great Britain. I was trying to decide between a sundress I'd seen in one of the windows in town or the cute shorts I'd probably get more use out of as she informed Zak that in 1893, the Kingdom of Hawai'i was overthrown, and Hawaii was a republic until 1898, when Congress officially annexed it, making it a territory and eventually a state in 1959.

"As interesting as this all sounds, I'd really like to get in a couple of hours of surfing," Levi interrupted.

"Of course. I'm sorry for going on and on," Malie apologized. "I have a habit of getting caught up in Hawaiian history."

"Which I found fascinating," Zak assured her. "Why don't you come to the house for dinner?" he invited her. "Bring Pono as well, if he gets out of jail."

"I'd like that." Malie smiled.

"Down, girl," Ellie whispered, in anticipation of the predictable arrival of Zoe the Jealous.

Chapter 7

By the time the gang and I had settled in to grill some steaks and watch the sun set, it felt like we had been on Maui for months. Could it have been only two and a half days? I felt bad about leaving Charlie for so long while we were in Lahaina, so I'd taken him for a long walk down the beach while the men surfed and Ellie took a nap. Malie had left in order to pick up Pono from the police station once he'd called to inform her that he'd been released. She promised to bring him over for dinner if he was willing to come so that we could all talk about what, if anything, to do next.

Our time in Lahaina had been somewhat productive. Not only had I bought three new outfits for my new baby sister, Harper, but I'd picked up a couple for myself as well. Ellie had treated herself to a new pair of flip-flops and Levi bought a couple of T-shirts. Zak claimed he didn't need anything but ended up sneaking away to buy me a pair of earrings with gold sea turtles dangling from gold posts that went with the necklace he'd bought me in Whalers Village.

Zak came over to sit down on the lounge behind me, positioning me between his legs and pulling me back so that I was leaning against his chest. I felt myself relax as his arms encircled my body and we both sat quietly watching the gentle surf roll toward shore. I love everything about Hawaii, but the evenings when the four of us relax and watch the sun set are turning out to be my favorite time of the day.

"Penny for your thoughts," Zak said after several minutes of communal silence.

"I was just thinking about what a good time I had shopping today," I responded. "Thank you again for the earrings." I touched the one on the left and twisted it between my fingers. "How was surfing?"

"It was fun. The waves were pretty mellow, but it's been a while since I've surfed, so that was probably just as well. I'd really like to go diving tomorrow if you're up for it."

"Always. I thought we could talk to Pono about the wreck Malie mentioned when he gets here. If they're still up for it, I'd love to go on a treasure hunt."

"Ellie said Malie called, and she and Pono will be here in a half hour or so. We can talk to them about it then. Did you ever call your mom?"

"I did."

"What?" Zak asked.

I turned and looked at him. How could he possibly know something was going on from my simple answer to his question?

"I can tell by your tone of voice that something is up," he said, as if he'd read my mind.

"It's probably nothing," I hedged.

Zak raised a single brow.

I repositioned my body so I was facing him. "Mom told me my dad was moving back into the guesthouse."

For those of you who don't know, my mom and dad aren't married, in spite of the fact that they have two daughters born twenty-five years apart. In fact, up until a few months ago, they'd never lived together. When my dad found out that my mom was pregnant with Harper, they'd decided to buy a property with both a main and a guesthouse so they could raise her together yet each have their own space. They insisted they weren't a couple, but I knew it was only a matter of time.

"Wasn't that the original plan?" Zak reminded me.

"Yeah, but after he moved into the main house toward the end of Mom's pregnancy and then stayed there for over two months after Harper was born, I thought he might make the main house his permanent residence."

"He probably just wanted to be around to help your mom with Harper during those first difficult months," Zak pointed out.

"I guess." I sighed. "I don't know what's wrong with those two. Everyone else can see that they love each other. Why don't they just get married and do away with the whole two-houses thing?"

Zak looked like he wanted to say something and then changed his mind. I watched as a myriad of emotions crossed his face before he finally spoke. "I guess people have their own timing when it comes to that type of thing. It'll happen. You just have to be patient, even when every day that you're patient eats away a bit of your soul."

"Eats away a bit of my soul? What's with the drama?" I teased.

"It's nothing." Zak shrugged. "So did you find out about the cat?"

"It turns out that the woman who lost her cat lives within a quarter mile of the campground where the dead squirrels have been turning up. My guess is that someone has left out poison for the animals. Jeremy is going to take Tank and Gunner there tomorrow and do a thorough search of the area."

"Who would do something like that?" Zak wondered.

"People can be pretty clueless. We had an incident a couple of years back. A homeowner had squirrels in his attic, so he mixed rat poison with sunflower seeds and left it out for them to eat. Not only did we find at least a dozen dead squirrels but two dogs in the area died as well. My guess is that something similar is going on now. I just hope we can find out who's responsible before any more animals turn up dead."

Zak pulled me back against his chest. "You're frustrated at being here when something like that is going on there."

Zak knew me so well. "A little," I admitted. "But I think it's important that we're here, and I really am having a good time in spite of the dead man in the pig pit."

Zak laughed. "One of the things I love about you is your ability to adapt to any situation."

"You know me; I'm the bendy type."

"Yes, you are," Zak growled. He leaned forward and kissed me on the neck.

"Zak," I scolded. "Malie and Pono will be here any minute. What will they think?"

"They'll think I want to make love to my hot girlfriend and they'll be right."

"Later," I promised.

The steaks were grilled to perfection, the Mai Tais delicious, and the salad fresh from the farmers market. The sun set over the water as we ate, lending an air of relaxation to an otherwise hectic day. No one had wanted to breach the subject of Pono's arrest until after the sky grew black and the fire in the pit on the deck was the only light in an otherwise dark night.

"The police are pretty sure I'm guilty," Pono said after Malie got the ball rolling by urging him to discuss the interview with the others. "I guess I get it. Everyone knows Anton and I didn't get along, and I'm sure someone must have seen us arguing. I suppose there are those who knew that I was alone at the pit after Keoke returned to the house."

Everyone sat very quietly.

"It would have been easy to do," Pono emphasized, "but I didn't do it," he clarified.

"Can you tell us about your argument with Anton?" I asked.

"We argued about the wreck, or at least the debris field of the wreck Malie and I found. I made the mistake of telling Leia, who used to treasure hunt with Malie and me. I thought she'd find it fascinating, and I guess she mentioned it to Anton. Anton warned me that diving in the area was dangerous, and that I should give up my search before I got both myself and Malie killed."

"Dangerous how?" Levi asked.

"Anton suggested that there might be certain persons engaging in illegal activities in the same area where we found the remnants."

"Drug runners," Ellie guessed.

"Probably, although Anton was intentionally vague. I told him that I'd lived in the area my whole life and wasn't going to let some haole tell me where I could and couldn't dive. He got angry and called me a few choice names that I was able to match quite nicely. I stormed off, and that's the last I ever saw of him."

"When was that?" I asked.

"I guess around eight-thirty or nine. It was a nice day and I really wasn't up for a party, so I left Keoke a note and went sailing."

"You left Keoke a note?" I said.

"Yeah. I went back to the house to let him know what I was going to do, but he was on the phone. I knew if I told my grandparents or sister that I'd decided to leave, they'd try to talk me out of it, so I wrote Keoke a quick note and left it in his room. I figured he'd see it when he went in to change his clothes."

"When we spoke to Keoke, he didn't mention a note," I pointed out. "In fact, he seemed as confused as anyone about your absence. Could someone have taken the note?"

Pono shrugged. "I guess. Keoke's bedroom door wasn't locked, but who would want to mess with the note?"

"Maybe the killer," Levi guessed. "If someone intended to set you up, they'd want everyone to think you remained on the island."

"For someone to have taken the note, they would have had to know you left it," Malie realized. "Did you see anyone when you went to Keoke's room?"

Pono thought about it. "There were people mingling about. Leia was in her room, but the door was open. She asked me if I'd seen Anton and I told her that I'd last seen him outside. I didn't mention the argument because I knew it would upset her."

"Anyone else?" I asked.

"That friend of Anton's was lurking in the hallway. I have no idea what he was up to and at the time it didn't seem relevant."

"Jeffrey?" I remembered the best man's name.

"Yeah, Jeffrey. I also remember seeing a couple of the caterers talking at the foot of the stairs. I don't know their names or what they were talking about, but I do remember thinking it was odd that they were in the main part of the house rather than the kitchen."

"Okay, so you saw Jeffrey, Leia, and two of the caterers. Did they see you?"

"I guess they did. The only one I spoke to was Leia."

"Can you think of anyone who would have gone into the room for any other reason?" I asked.

"I suppose the maid might have gone in to check on things. Like I said, the room wasn't locked, so anyone could have gone in there and taken the note."

"You said you argued with Anton about the treasure hunt. Did Keoke know about it?" I asked.

Pono looked at Malie.

"I didn't tell him," she insisted.

"I didn't either. Keoke's dad had the fever. It nearly destroyed his family, and in the end it cost him his life. Keoke would have told us to forget about looking for the treasure. I didn't want to argue with him, so I didn't tell him, although I suppose if he heard Anton and me arguing, he must know now. I'm afraid our conversation got pretty heated. It most likely would have ended in a physical altercation if Jeffrey hadn't come along and encouraged Anton to head back to the house."

"What do you think we should do at this point?" Malie asked.

"I think we should forget about Anton and go diving like we planned," Pono answered. "The cops will figure out that I didn't kill him. I'm sure once they do, they'll put more effort into tracking down the real killer. We may lose the wreck if we don't find it before the next big storm, so I say let the cops do their job and we'll do ours."

Malie didn't say anything.

"Come on, Mal," Pono coaxed. "You know I'm right. Anton is dead and nothing we do will change that. I don't think Leia will be open to our help at this point, so really, why should we get involved?"

"Okay. When do you want to go diving?" Malie asked.

"Tomorrow," Pono decided.

"I'm in. How about you guys?" Malie looked at us.

"Is it okay with you?" I asked Pono.

"If we find a treasure, it belongs to Malie and me."

"Agreed," I answered for the group.

"Let's meet in the morning. The marina at seven?"

"Sounds good," I said, although I secretly wished he would have opted for a much later start time.

Chapter 8

Monday, June 30

There is nothing that can quite compare to lying on the deck of a dive boat after a full day of diving and letting the sun soak the fatigue from your limbs. Of course, the cold beer Pono had thought to bring helped to relieve the tenderness of muscles that had not enjoyed this particular activity for quite some time.

It had been a productive day. Ellie had stayed on the boat with Charlie while the rest of us went down several times. Pono schooled us on what to do and what to look for. I'd managed to retrieve half a plate that appeared to be fairly old, a hairbrush that looked to be too modern to have any significance, and a coin that was so covered in sea crud that it was impossible to identify. Zak had a little better luck, with the discovery of a silver bracelet and a knife with a silver handle. Levi was too busy chasing fish to find much of anything, but he did manage to come up with a large object that was shaped roughly like a cross but was covered in barnacles that Pono assured us could be soaked off. Malie found a number of items, including a gold locket that at one time might have held a valued photo, several pieces of silverware with initials on the handles, and a ceramic pitcher. Pono found a heavy chain that at one time must have held something down or possibly supported an anchor, and a cannonball with an emblem stamped onto one side.

"Did you see those sharks circling overhead when we were down by the reef?" Malie asked.

"I did. They were so beautiful." I smiled.

"You saw sharks?" Ellie screeched.

"Just a couple of reef sharks," I said.

"In the water with you?"

Pono laughed. "Don't worry; this particular breed hardly ever eats humans. They're nocturnal feeders that were probably just chillin'."

"*Hardly ever* eats humans?" Ellie gasped. I thought she was going to pass out.

"You do realize that we're in the ocean, right?" I reminded her. "Sharks live in the ocean, and you'll occasionally run into one, if you're lucky."

"*Lucky?*"

"We weren't in any danger," Levi assured her. "Sharks respond to sound vibrations. You're probably more likely to get bit flapping around on the surface while you snorkel than we were while diving."

I kicked Levi. Hard.

"Ouch. Why'd you do that?"

I nodded toward Ellie, who was completely pale.

"Oh," Levi said as he rubbed his shin.

"What is that island in the distance?" Zak asked.

I was grateful for the change in subject.

"Kahoʻolawe," Pono told him.

"Is it inhabited?" I asked.

"Not currently, although it has been in the past. During World War II, Kahoʻolawe was used as a training ground and bombing range by the armed forces. After decades of protests, live-fire training exercises were terminated, and the Kahoʻolawe Island Reserve was established. Today, the island can be used only for native Hawaiian cultural, spiritual, and subsistence purposes," Malie explained.

"And before the armed forces took over?"

"There is a long history of small settlements on the island," Malie said. "Sometime around the year 1000, Kahoʻolawe was settled by native Hawaiians, and small, temporary fishing communities were established along the coast. War among competing chiefs caused a decrease in population. During the War of Kamokuhi, the ruler of the Big Island raided Kahoʻolawe in an unsuccessful attempt to take Maui from the King of Maui, which devastated the local population even further. I'm not sure of all the details surrounding the island population, but I do know that the island was mostly deserted during the 1700s. After the arrival of missionaries in the 1800s, the Kingdom of Hawaii replaced the death penalty with exile, and Kahoʻolawe became a men's penal colony sometime around 1830."

"Wow, that's really interesting."

"You should talk to my Uncle Rory," Malie suggested. "He knows a lot more about local history than I do."

"Speaking of Rory, maybe he can help us identify some of this stuff," Pono said. "If we can identify the marking on the cannonball, maybe we can trace it back to a specific ship."

"So do we take tomorrow off and go to my uncle's in the hope that we can find these marks in one of his books, or do we come out again and keep looking?" Malie asked.

Pono sat quietly as he considered her question. I honestly didn't care about the answer—either activity seemed interesting to me—so I closed my eyes and let the motion of the boat lull me toward the most relaxed state I'd been in for quite some time. Charlie was asleep under the lounge chair I was lying on. I wasn't sure how he'd do with the day-long trip, but he seemed to enjoy being with everyone, and I knew he'd hate being left at the house alone. We'd anchored around midday and used the lifeboat to make the short trip onto a nearby island, where we'd eaten our lunch and let Charlie run around a bit. I wasn't certain that Pono would be thrilled to have Charlie aboard his boat, but when I asked about bringing him, he'd smiled and responded that having a dog on board could only bring them good luck. His attitude made me like him even more.

"I suppose you could take the artifacts and pay a visit to your uncle, and maybe the guys and I could dive again tomorrow," Pono suggested after he'd thought about it a bit.

"That's fine with me," Malie said. "I really need to stop off to check on the turtles we're monitoring on the south shore. Would you girls like to go along with me to my uncle's? He lives on the south end of the island, so it's about a ninety-minute drive from where you're staying."

"I would," Ellie answered.

I could feel Ellie looking at me as she waited for my reply.

"Zoe?" Ellie asked.

"Hmm," I responded.

"I think that was a yes." Ellie laughed. "Do you really think we found something?"

"It's hard to say," Malie answered truthfully. "The items we found are old and most likely came from a shipwreck, but until we find the body of a ship, or something so definitive as to positively identify a ship, it's hard to say if these items will lead us anywhere. It's fun to look, though."

"Yeah, it really is," Ellie agreed. "But," she added, "as fun as this has been, I'm starving. We have a ton of food back at the house. If we're done here, why don't we all head back and I'll make something? That is, if you and Pono would like to join us."

"Ellie is a great cook." I opened my eyes and sat up. "She even owns her own restaurant back in Ashton Falls."

"You do?" Malie asked. "Why have you never mentioned that?"

"I guess it didn't come up in conversation," Ellie said. "And it's not a fine-dining restaurant. It's a soup-and-sandwich place on the beach. Very causal."

"It's an extremely popular place to eat," I clarified. "Ellie is being modest. Her appetizers are famous and her desserts . . . let's just say that you haven't tasted heaven until you've tried one of Ellie's special desserts."

Malie laughed. "I think you've been holding out on us. I'd love to come for dinner. Pono?"

"Any day someone else cooks for me is a good day."

"Can I help?" Malie asked.

"I'd love that." Ellie smiled.

"I guess we should head back," Pono said. "It'll take a while to dock, and I for one would love to stop by my place to shower and change before I come over."

"I'd love to see the other things you found before we came along," Levi said. "Maybe you could bring them?"

"I could do that."

"Can we bring anything else?" Malie asked. "Maybe something to contribute to the meal?"

"I think I have everything we need," Ellie said. "Although I'd love to learn to make some traditional Hawaiian dishes while I'm here."

"I have some recipes that were handed down by my grandmother. I'm not much of a cook myself, but I'd be happy to share them. I'll bring them tonight, and you can look through them and copy any you find interesting. Zoe said you are famous for your appetizers. We have a local favorite called a musubi."

"What's in it?"

"It's basically spam and sticky rice wrapped in nori, a seaweed wrap used for sushi. It sounds strange, I'm sure, but it's really good."

"Spam? As in the stuff you get in a can?" Ellie asked.

Malie laughed. "Spam is a staple in Hawaii. Don't knock it until you've tried it."

"I'll try anything once. Maybe when we get back we can have a luau at Zak's and invite all our friends. I can try out some of the traditional Hawaiian dishes I plan to learn to make," Ellie suggested.

"No pig," I insisted.

"I think we can do without the pig. At least a whole pig. But maybe we can serve some pork dishes instead."

"We have a dish called Kalua pork that is really good. I'm pretty sure I have a recipe for it. You can also do pork and pineapple kabobs. They would be fun to make, and to try some of my grandmother's recipes while you are here. My mom died a long time ago, and there are many dishes I haven't had since my grandma died over eight years ago."

"We'll plan a day," Ellie promised.

"Not to interrupt, but do either of you recognize that boat?" I asked Malie and Pono. "It's been following us for the past ten minutes."

Malie squinted. "It's pretty far away, but it sort of looks like the yacht that was in the harbor a while back."

Pono got out a pair of binoculars and took a closer look. "I think it *is* the yacht that was in the harbor. I thought they'd left the area."

"Do you think it's the drug runners Anton warned you about?" Malie sounded nervous.

"If these guys are drug runners, they're a different breed of drug runner than any I've ever seen before. Take a look."

Pono handed the binoculars to Malie, who then handed them to me. The men were all dressed in expensive suits. They looked like mobsters rather than drug runners and seemed to be arguing about something, although they were much too far away to hear what they were saying. One of the men raised his arm to point at something in the distance. I could see the sun reflect off something that looked a whole lot like a gun strapped to his chest.

"Let's get out of here," I said.

I suddenly began to wonder if taking Anton's warning about the danger involved in our treasure hunt might not be a good idea after all.

"You know what I find odd?" I asked as the six of us dined on tri-tip, fresh corn on the cob, avocado and tomato salad, and flaky French bread.

"What do you find odd?" Ellie asked.

"The timing of Anton's murder. If I had a grudge against him and wanted to kill him, why would I do it on an island with limited access and a finite number of guests? Why not do it the day before or the day after the party, when the number of potential suspects would be greatly increased?"

"Maybe Anton's death wasn't premeditated," Zak pointed out. "Maybe the murder was a crime of passion."

"Or maybe the killer saw Anton and Pono arguing and realized they had the perfect opportunity to kill Anton and frame Pono," Malie presented.

"Or maybe the killer didn't have access to Anton during the course of his everyday life but knew he'd have an opportunity at the luau. He was a busy man with a layer of people who served as watchdogs that protected him from the general public," Pono added.

"What do you mean?" I asked.

"Say the killer was one of the caterers or plantation workers, or the gardener at the estate. Unless this person knew Anton personally, the chance of gaining access to him was remote. There's a security guard at the building where he worked. If you got past him—and few people ever did—you still needed to get past his secretary . . . who, I might add, is a barracuda in a sensible skirt. Anton lived in a secure building with a metal detector and a security guard. His apartment is in the penthouse, which requires a special key to access. It'd be easier to get to the Pope."

"So I want to kill Anton and find out that he will be on the island and recognize that as my chance?" I put together.

"Makes sense," Levi agreed.

"Okay, but why dispose of the body in such a public way?" I asked. "If the murder was a crime of opportunity, why not just bury the body or dump it in the ocean? Why the pig pit?"

"You think the public display is significant," Malie said to me.

"It makes sense that it is. Who would not only want to kill him but send a statement as well?"

Everyone sat quietly as we pondered the question. The surf was gentle tonight. The moon had risen and the trail of light that reflected off the water held my gaze. There was a warm breeze fluttering through the palm trees, creating a primal rhythm that reminded me of the call of the native drums I'd heard coming from the distance at night.

"Anton was stabbed in the back," I pointed out. "Stabbing someone in the back could just be opportunistic, but it could have been ritualistic as well. Is there anyone who might feel that Anton stabbed them in the back? Someone he might have betrayed?"

"James Pope," Malie and Pono said in unison.

"James Pope?" I asked.

"James and Anton used to be partners," Malie began. "They did several deals together and planned to work on a development on the southeast coast, near Hana. The area is environmentally sensitive, so they were faced with a series of roadblocks that pretty much killed the project. I'm not sure what happened exactly, but the next thing I knew, Anton had partnered up with a local businessman named Noa Rees, who is well regarded and has a lot of pull with the local government. The men planned a project in almost same exact area where Anton and James were shot down, but this time it looked like the permit was going to be approved. James took Anton to court, but Anton somehow managed to convince the judge that the project he was developing with Noa was a completely different project from the one he'd planned with James, even though everyone knew he'd simply repackaged the original plans."

"So Anton symbolically stabbed James in the back. Was he at the party?" I asked.

"No," Pono said.

"Is Noa still working with Anton?"

"No. Anton had a new partner named Kingsley Portman," Pono told them.

"Actually, I think Kingsley and Anton have worked together for a long time," Malie corrected him. "Kingsley lives on the mainland and so is more of a silent partner, but it seems like he's been around a lot lately, so I'm guessing he's more involved in the current project."

"Can you think of any reason Kingsley would want Anton out of the way?" I asked.

Malie and Pono both shook their heads.

"So we're back to square one," Ellie decided. "Anyone want dessert?"

I helped Zak clear the table while Levi and Pono built a fire in the pit and Ellie and Malie prepared the dessert. The complex murder mystery we faced was giving me a headache, and I found myself agreeing with Pono that we should drop the whole thing and focus on the treasure hunt. I didn't know the players in the murder well enough to offer anything beyond what the local police were likely to turn up, so why should I put myself through the mental exercise?

By the time Zak and I had finished the dishes, Pono was playing the ukulele next to the fire while Levi, Ellie, and Malie sipped wine and nibbled on Ellie's pineapple coconut cake.

"How about you and I sneak out and go for a walk?" Zak whispered.

A walk did sound nice, and we really hadn't had much alone time since we'd been on Maui.

"I should tell Ellie," I said. "If she realizes we're gone, she might worry, given her mental state and the events of the past few days."

"I'll grab our sweatshirts," Zak offered. "Do you want your red one?"

"Yeah, that's fine, and get Charlie's leash. We might as well take him out for his evening constitutional."

After I explained to the others what we were going to do, Zak, Charlie, and I headed down the beach. We let the dog run free since the beach was mostly deserted at that time of night. As we walked along the sand, Pono's ukulele faded into the background.

"It sure is beautiful tonight." I linked my hand with Zak's.

"Most nights on the island are pretty spectacular."

"And I had fun diving today. I hope we can figure out what ship the debris field is from. Not that I care about the treasure per se, but finding it would make for a good story to tell when we get back home."

"I have to say this trip has been a lot more eventful than I'd imagined it would be. I'm enjoying myself, but I do miss having *us* time."

"Yeah," I agreed.

"Maybe we can go to dinner tomorrow? Just the two of us. I know a great seafood place on the other side of the island. They have an extensive wine list and the deck is right on the water."

"I'm going with Malie to the south shore tomorrow," Zoe reminded him. "Maybe later in the week?"

"It's Fourth of July weekend. I know you and Ellie have been making plans for the four of us. I guess we can try to sneak away next week."

"Wow, I can't believe it's already the Fourth of July. I should call Jeremy to remind him to run our annual pets and fireworks article in the paper."

"I'm sure Jeremy will remember."

"I know, but I should remind him. Jeremy's a night owl, so I'm sure he's still up. I could call his cell so he can do it first thing in the morning. Besides, I wanted to talk to him some more about the

poisonings near the campground. I've been thinking .
. ."

Zak stopped walking. He turned me so that we were standing face-to-face. I stopped talking as he looked deeply into my eyes. I was certain he was going to kiss me, but then he simply pulled me close and held me tight. We stood that way for several minutes, his arms around my body, my ear pressed to his chest. I could hear the rhythm of his heart beat as I relaxed into his embrace. The longer we stood perfectly still, the calmer and less cluttered my mind became. I know that Zak loves me for who I am, but I also realize that more often than not, I'm a mental and emotional mess. I seem to be the type of person who's involved in everything and with everybody, all of the time. Zak deserves to have his own special Zoe time.

I let myself concentrate on Zak's beating heart as thoughts of sunken treasure, dead bodies, poisoned animals, and Fourth of July plans faded into the recesses of my mind. I could feel the warm water swirl around my ankles as the tide came in. I lifted my head and kissed Zak's neck as the outgoing tide pulled the sand around my toes into the sea.

"It's a nice night for a swim," I whispered into Zak's ear.

"I thought we might stay out a while longer."

"I wasn't thinking about a swim in the pool," I said as I pulled both my sweatshirt and T-shirt over my head.

Chapter 9

Tuesday, July 1

I woke up at first light the next morning. Zak was still snoring softly and there was no movement in the rest of the house to indicate that anyone else was up yet either. I decided to take Charlie for a walk down the beach to clear my mind. The walk with Zak the previous evening had been nice. Okay, better than nice. The problem was that one thing had led to another, and I'd barely gotten any sleep. Some people do fine on a couple of hours a night, but I'm not one of them. I had a feeling it was going to be a long day.

I watched as Charlie trotted along, chasing waves. I wasn't sure how he would do with the waves crashing onto the shore, but he seemed to be having the time of his life. Zak had even put him on the front of his stand-up paddleboard yesterday and taken him for a short ride near the shore. Charlie had sat perfectly still, not seeming to mind being confined to the small board at all. He was good for Zak. I know he can't replace Lambda in Zak's heart, but it was evident that Charlie's loyalty and devotion to him was helping him heal.

I thought about my relationship with Zak during the past few months. I realized that Charlie had been much more conscientious when it came to the whole devotion thing than me. I'd been so busy since the Zoo reopened and with all the murders and friends in crisis. . . . The more I thought about it, the more certain I was that Zak had been there all along, waiting in the sidelines for me to finally have a moment to devote entirely to him.

Sure, we had stolen moments here and there, but stolen moments really were all they boiled down to. We'd gone to New York together, but that had been a business trip, and Zak had been tied up most of the time. I know that Zak had been hoping to find a little us time in Maui while we were away from our daily lives in Ashton Falls. He'd been there for me every step of the way, in good times and bad, through friends in crisis and animals in jeopardy, and never once had he asked me for anything.

I considered turning around and heading back to the house. Maybe Zak was still asleep and I could wake him with an intimate caress. Then I remembered that I never had talked to Jeremy, and if I didn't call him this morning and he *had* forgotten to run the feature on the effect of fireworks on the mental health of our canine friends, we'd most likely miss the deadline.

I took out my cell and dialed. Although it was barely dawn in Hawaii, it would be midmorning in Ashton Falls. I watched a pair of divers with spearguns enter the water as I waited for Jeremy to pick up. I knew that whatever they caught would be offered for sale in a few hours at neighborhood markets. That was another thing I really loved about Hawaii: there were stands selling fresh seafood and produce on practically every corner.

"Hey, Jeremy, it's Zoe," I greeted as Jeremy picked up.

"How's the trip?"

"It's really great. Say, did you remember to submit the Fourth of July article we run every year to the paper?"

"Did it yesterday."

Zak was right; it could have waited.

"I figured."

"Is something wrong?" Jeremy asked. "You seem sort of down."

I sighed. "No, everything is fine. How are the Bryton Lake dogs?"

"They all seem to be fine. Scott is going to come by this afternoon, but he thinks we can start taking applications by the end of the week."

"Excellent. And the squirrels?"

Jeremy paused before answering. "Are you sure you're okay?"

"Just tired, I guess."

I could almost picture Jeremy's shrug. He was always willing to lend an ear but not one to push.

"We did a pretty careful search of the area where the dead squirrels have been found and didn't find anything that might indicate intentional poisoning. We did, however, find additional victims of whatever it is that's going on."

"Victims?"

"A half dozen squirrels, a raccoon, a couple of birds, and a coyote. Scott also notified us that he'd had two sick cats and a sick dog brought in. All of them seemed to be suffering from some sort of toxic reaction, but he couldn't isolate what the specific cause might be. I called Salinger after I completed my investigation and convinced him to quarantine the area. The owner of the campground, as well as the folks who were camping, weren't happy. It's the Fourth of July this weekend, and every campground in the area is booked to capacity. Salinger finally settled on a compromise: the campers who want to stay are being allowed to do it at their own risk. So far we haven't had any human victims, so requiring the campground to close did seem premature. He's allowed us to run a feature in the newspaper, and to put up posters warning people to keep their pets away from the area."

"The fact that we have dead squirrels *and* dogs *and* birds really worries me. There are things that are toxic to specific species, but for there to be such a wide range of victims, I'm thinking it has to be poison."

"Tank and I are going to look again," Jeremy promised. "And we'll keep looking until we figure out what's going on."

"Have you gone door-to-door to question residents in the area?" I asked. "Maybe someone has seen something that can explain this."

"Not yet, but we will. I want you to relax and have fun. Let Tiffany and me handle this. If there's something to be found, we'll find it."

"Is there anything else I should be aware of?" I asked.

Jeremy hesitated.

"Just tell me," I instructed.

"Are you sure you want to know? You already seem a little grouchy."

"I'm not grouchy," I insisted, even thought I was and I knew it. I really should have tried to go back to sleep instead of taking this walk. The lack of zzzz was obviously getting to me.

"The county has decided to do an inspection," Jeremy blurted.

"What? Why?"

"I don't know; they just sent a certified letter and said that an annual review was part of our permit."

"We've only been open for four months," I argued.

"I know. And I realize it's a hassle. But is it really that big a deal?"

"Of course it's a big deal," I snapped. "Sorry," I said immediately. "It's not your fault. I'm sure someone complained about something and the county feels they need to check it out. When is it?"

"Soon," Jeremy answered vaguely.

"How soon?"

"Thursday."

"This Thursday?" I felt myself begin to hyperventilate.

"It'll be fine. The Zoo is great. We're following every requirement the county tacked onto our permit."

"They'll be looking for something specific," I pointed out. "Did they indicate what?"

"No. The letter is simply a notification of date and time."

"Okay." I sighed. Just what I didn't need: one more thing to worry about. "Scan and e-mail me the letter. I'll see what I can find out."

"Do you remember how you made me a manager?" Jeremy said. "You put me on salary and gave me medical benefits and paid for Morgan's delivery as a bonus."

"Yeah. So?"

"Let me be a manager. I can handle this. You just need to let me do it."

I hesitated.

"Please. If you won't let me handle this simple inspection, then I don't know what I'm doing here."

Jeremy was right. I was micromanaging and I had no reason to. Jeremy was an excellent employee, capable of handling whatever came up.

"Okay," I said.

"Really? Thanks, Zoe. I won't let you down."

By the time I got back to the house, Zak and Levi were already gone. Ellie had made a pot of coffee and was sitting by the pool sipping from a white ceramic mug. She looked tired, but she had a smile on her face as she watched a school of dolphins playing in the water.

"Coffee?" she asked

"Thanks." I poured myself a mug after refilling Charlie's water dish.

"Malie called. She's going to pick us up at around eleven. She thought it would be nice to stop for lunch on the way to her uncle's."

"I guess I should head in for a shower after I finish my coffee."

"And Rob called," Ellie added. "He's in Ashton Falls, packing up his things."

"Yeah, I heard," I admitted.

"He wanted to know what to do with the stuff I'd left at his house."

I waited quietly for her to continue.

"I really thought I'd have a chance to see Hannah one more time, but he said he plans to be gone before we get home."

A single tear slid down Ellie's cheek.

"Maybe that's for the best." I placed my hand over hers.

She took a deep breath. "Maybe. Part of me wants to have the opportunity to say good-bye to Hannah, but I suppose seeing her again would make everything all that much harder."

"Yeah," I said. "I think it would."

"I did realize something while I was talking to Rob, though. Something important."

"What's that?"

"I'm pretty sure I never really loved him. I wanted to love him. It made everything so much more convenient, but while I was talking to him, I realized I wasn't sad at all that he was walking out of my life. I've been sitting here for the past hour thinking about things, and I believe I've come to the conclusion that they've worked out just the way they should. If Hannah's mother—her real mother—" Ellie emphasized, "wants to be back in her life, then she should."

"Yeah," I agreed.

"My relationship with Rob has helped me realize how badly I want to be a mother. I mean, I was willing to marry a man I didn't love to gain a daughter I'd grown to love."

"You're only twenty-five," I reminded Ellie. "There's plenty of time to find the right man and be a mother."

"Maybe."

Ellie sat quietly and looked out at the ocean. Then she tucked her legs up under her body and sipped her beverage. "The thing is," she continued after several minutes, "that the longer I sit here thinking about finding a guy in order to have the child my heart longs for, the firmer it is in my mind that I don't really need a man to have a child."

I laughed. "I realize it's been a while since high-school biology, but you actually do need a man."

Ellie grinned. "What I meant was that I only need to *borrow* a man. I don't actually need to marry a man in order to have a child. The single parents group is full of parents who are raising children alone. If they can do it, so can I."

"Maybe," I acknowledged, "but I think having a child with a man you love and want to spend your life with would be much more fulfilling than just going to some clinic and having the sperm of a nameless, faceless donor implanted into your uterus."

"The donor doesn't have to be nameless and faceless," Ellie pointed out. "I saw a thing on the Internet where a woman ran an ad for donors and interviewed them personally before choosing the one she thought would make the best biological father for her baby."

"Really? You're going to run an ad and interview men about donating sperm? It seems a little cold. And creepy," I added. "These men would know who you were and where you lived. Trust me, running an ad is not the way to go."

Ellie shrugged but didn't look convinced.

"Promise me you'll think more about this before you do anything."

Ellie didn't answer.

I adjusted my position so that I was looking directly into her eyes. "I know you're hurting. I know Hannah left a hole in your heart that you're desperate to fill. But please give it some time before you do anything you might end up regretting."

Ellie bit her lip.

"Promise me," I said persuasively.

"But . . ."

"If you wait at least three months from today to do anything and still want to go this route, I'll help you in any way I can, but please promise me you'll give this some serious thought."

"Three months?"

"Yeah. Today is July 1. If you still want to explore this option on October 1, I'll drive you to a clinic, help you interview men, whatever it is that needs to be done. Agreed?"

"Agreed."

Chapter 10

Ellie, Malie, and I decided to treat ourselves to lunch at the Grand Wailea Resort on our way south to meet Malie's uncle. I had won a gift card that was good for any of the restaurants at the resort as part of my humiliation gift package. As we pulled into the drive, I knew it was all worth it. Talk about a decadent vacation experience. Situated on forty acres fronting spectacular Wailea Beach, the resort had several pools, including one featuring four slides, a sand beach, six waterfalls, caves, and a swim-up bar. Although there were a number of restaurants to choose from, we selected one that offered fantastic views and a casual dining menu. I had a hard time deciding between the grilled ahi sandwich and the island fish tacos but eventually went with the tacos. Ellie had lobster salad croissant sliders, while Malie chose a seared ahi poke wrap. Everything was delicious.

"This place is really something," I commented as I looked out onto the meticulously landscaped grounds. The crystal-clear pools were surrounded by perfectly manicured lawns and flowers of every variety imaginable.

"It's a very popular resort with visitors from the mainland," Malie said. "Personally, I find the area a bit too commercial, but it's fun to have a spa day every now and then, and I hear the golf course is world-class. I have a friend who had her bachelorette party here and we really did have a good time. The dining is fantastic, the spa services extensive, and the beach one of the best in the area. There is also a fitness center and tennis courts that are quite nice."

"I bet the rooms are spectacular." Ellie sighed. "It would be a dream come true to wake up to an ocean view every morning."

"You do wake up to an ocean view," I pointed out, "at least while we're here."

Ellie giggled. "True. I guess I'm just getting caught up in the romance of it all."

"We had the party in one of the villas," Malie informed us. "It was pretty spectacular. Still, I have to side with Zoe on this one. However wonderful this place is, it doesn't compare to the house you're staying in on the north shore. What I wouldn't give to live in that house."

"You could always marry Keoke," Ellie teased.

Malie blushed. "Keoke and I are just friends."

Based on Malie's blush, I'd say Ellie hadn't been all that far off in her suggestion that Malie might be interested in our host.

"Does anyone have room for dessert?" Malie asked. "They have a fantastic selection. Perhaps we can share something."

"I'm game," Ellie chimed in.

"Me too."

We took another look at the menu and decided to share two offerings: pineapple upside-down cake glazed with Myers's Rum and a brownie sundae made with an Oreo crust.

After we ate, we took a quick tour of the grounds. The intricate network of pools, the lush gardens, and the fantastic location were enough to convince me that a romantic getaway with Zak was going to have to be scheduled in the near future. The three of us asked a couple who were sitting and chatting on a bench near the entrance to take a photo of us, which I immediately posted to my Facebook page. My friends and family at home would be happy to see Ellie smiling and having such a good time.

We continued to travel south after we left the resort. The drive was breathtaking as the lush landscape gave way to an area that was both barren and remote.

"This is where we turn off to the area's black sand beach, if you'd like to take a look," Malie offered.

"The sand is black?" Ellie asked.

"Yes. Unlike typical sand, which is made up of ground coral and shells, black sand is ground lava that turns hard at the water's edge. It isn't the best beach for sunbathing, but it's a good place to snorkel or dive; not only is there abundant sea life but green sea turtles are drawn here as well."

"Let's stop on the way back. I'd like to try snorkeling, but I'd hate to be late to meet your uncle."

"Sounds like a plan." Malie continued down the road.

Malie's uncle lived at the end of a dirt road off the main highway. The house, a large two-story colonial with single-story wings on either side, was built of red brick, and each of the nine large windows gracing the main structure was framed with shiny black shutters. Atop the rooftops of the wings were a series of dormers with pane windows and artistic trim. Lush green lawns, densely planted flowerbeds, and hundreds if not thousands of dark red roses surrounded the building.

"Wow, your uncle's house is fantastic," I complimented.

"I'll take you on a tour," Malie offered. "I'm sure Uncle Rory won't mind. In fact, he may offer to do it himself. He loves to show off all the furniture and artwork he's collected in his travels."

We walked up the seven steps to the front door and rang the bell. A tall, thin woman in a tidy maid's uniform answered.

"Malie," she said, hugging her warmly. "It's been so long since you've been to visit."

"I know, Maggie. I guess I've been busy. We'll catch up later. These are my friends, Zoe and Ellie." She pointed to each of us in turn. "We've come to talk to Uncle Rory about a shipwreck we hope to find."

"He'll love that. A fair warning, though," Maggie said, smiling at Ellie and me, "once you get him started talking, you may not be able to get him to stop. Rory does love an audience. I think I saw him heading toward the library a little while ago."

"Thanks. I'll look for him there." Malie hugged the woman one more time before we headed down a long hallway.

The room we entered was unlike any home library I'd ever seen. Thousands of books were stacked on mahogany shelves that were arranged along all four walls on two levels. The first-level shelves were about six feet tall, with two sets of stairs, one on each end of the room, leading to the second-level stacks. The ceiling was high, allowing the two stories to be open to each other. In the center of the room on the bottom level was a long hardwood table surrounded with hardwood chairs. The room was spectacular, but in my opinion the most spectacular feature of all was a grand old desk and a red leather chair tucked into a large bay window overlooking the rocky shore of the Pacific Ocean.

"Uncle Rory," Malie greeted a jolly-looking older man who appeared to be in his late seventies. "These are the friends I was telling you about."

"I'm happy to meet you both."

"Your home is gorgeous," I said.

"Thank you. I am very proud of what I have created. It has taken me many years to get it just right."

Rory hugged Malie. "I'm so sorry to hear about Anton."

Malie hugged Rory back. She'd admitted to us on the way over that her uncle had never really liked Anton, but he appeared to care very much for his niece.

"Is there anything I can do?" he asked.

"To be honest, I'd like to forget about Anton's murder and focus on the relics. The more I talk about it, the more the whole thing seems to affect me."

"Certainly. Please have a seat. Let's take a look at what you've brought."

Malie emptied the bag she'd brought onto the surface of the table.

Rory picked up the first item and began to examine it. He made a few notes on a yellow legal pad and then picked up the next piece. He quietly and methodically examined each item before setting it aside. I could see this was going to take a while, so I asked if it was okay to look around.

Rory's collection of books was more than impressive. There were first editions of James Joyce's *Ulysses*, as well as a copy of *A Portrait of the Artist as a Young Man*. It looked as though he had a complete set of Dickens, as well as complete sets of several Russian authors, including Dostoevsky and Tolstoy. The thing that struck me as the most awesome was that Uncle Rory seemed to have a wide range of books, from modern mysteries to valuable classics and beautiful poetry volumes by such authors as Walt Whitman and Emily Dickenson.

"Your collection is fantastic," I commented as I removed a leather-bound book with yellowed pages from a shelf and opened it to find a handwritten dedication.

"You like old books?" Rory asked.

"I'm not a collector. As a matter of fact, I've never even read most of the wonderful books you've so carefully assembled. But I do have an appreciation for literature. It must have taken you years to collect all of this.

"Generations, actually. My grandfather and father were both collectors. Some of these books belonged to my grandfather's grandfather. I treasure each and every one as if they were my own children. Come, let me show you a few of my favorites."

Rory got up and walked over to a locked cabinet. He removed a book.

"This is a signed copy of *The Longest Day* by Cornelius Ryan. It's a first edition signed by the author to Eleanor Roosevelt. It says, 'To Mrs. Eleanor

Roosevelt, whose husband nearly led the way to victory.'"

"Wow, it must be worth a fortune."

"Maybe not a fortune, but it is among my most prized possessions. I also have quite a few less valuable but still dearly loved books on Hawaiian history, as well as a signed copy of *The Catcher in the Rye*. It is not as old as some of the others but treasured all the same. And I have a first edition of Walt Whitman's *Leaves of Grass*, as well as a copy of the final edition of that work, which is referred to as the deathbed edition."

"Which is your favorite?" I asked.

"Actually, my favorite is a magazine rather than a book."

Rory unlocked a glass cabinet and took out an old *Life* magazine. "This is one of five million copies of the first publication of *Old Man and the Sea*."

"I thought *Old Man and the Sea* was a book."

"It was, but it was also featured in the magazine."

"I think I found something," Malie interrupted from the table, where Rory had left her to look through old shipping journals. "It looks like the initials on the silverware we found are the same as the ones found in this old photo."

Rory returned to the table. He pulled out a small magnifying glass and looked closely at a photo of recovered items from a British freighter that sailed in the early 1800s. "You know, they found that wreck not all that far from the area where you were diving. It was ten—no, twelve years ago—but I suppose there are still things down there that have never been recovered. If this is from the same ship, what you probably found is drift. Where exactly did you say you were diving?"

"South of Maui, near Kahoʻolawe."

"Malie told us you knew a lot about the history of the island," I said.

"Yes, Kahoʻolawe has a rich history I find fascinating. For native Hawaiians, Kahoʻolawe is a sacred island, deeply rooted in our culture and religion. In ancient times, the island was inhabited by people who made their living mainly by fishing and farming. Indications of these early times can be found in the carved petroglyphs, or drawings, on the flat surfaces of the rocks. Some of the oldest and largest Hawaiian shrines are located on Kahoʻolawe. I have a book about the island, if you are interested."

"I'm only on the island for a short time."

Rory got up and took a book from a high shelf. "Take it and look it over. You can give it to Malie to return when you leave."

"Thank you," I said, accepting the old tome. "I really appreciate this."

"I enjoy finding one as young as you with a love of history. I find it a rarity these days."

If I were going to be honest, I'd have to tell him I wasn't as much of a history lover as Uncle Rory assumed, but believing this to be true seemed to make him happy, so I didn't say anything.

"So about the relics . . ." Malie said.

The elderly man returned to the table, picked up one of the items, and looked at his notes. I could tell by the way he moved that he was a deliberate person who wouldn't be hurried.

"It looks as if you have items from more than a single vessel," he began after studying each item carefully. "While the silverware is English, the coin is clearly Spanish, and the mark on this knife . . ."

Rory held up the knife and looked at it more closely. "I'd like to keep a few of these items for a day or two so that I can do additional research."

"I'm sure that will be fine with Pono," Malie said. "Do you think we have anything?"

Rory hesitated. He picked up one of the cannonballs and rolled it between his hands. "You just might."

Chapter 11

Wednesday July 2

"So how's the trip going?" my dad asked the next morning. I'd returned from my morning run and was relaxing by the pool. It was another beautiful day in paradise as the bright sun reflected on the waves crashing into shore. The surf report mentioned that we were due for a couple of days of larger than normal swells, so Levi and Zak had both opted to hit the water for a few hours before we were supposed to meet up with Pono and Malie, who had decided to attend the hearing Anton's partner, Kingsley, had arranged regarding the real estate development they'd wanted to build on the north shore.

"It's been really fun," I said. "We've been busy diving for buried treasure."

"Do tell."

I filled my dad in on the dive we'd made on Monday and the relics we'd found. "Ellie and I went to the south shore yesterday with Malie, the woman who told us about the suspected wreck. Her uncle is some big historian. You should see the library in his house. It's bigger than the public library in Ashton Falls. And talk about elegant. It's two stories tall, with an open-beam ceiling and thousands of books of every genre and language. You would love it."

"It sounds wonderful," Dad agreed.

"Rory has tons of old books about all the different ships that sailed in the area centuries ago. I have no idea how he knew which books to look for, but he seemed to know just what we'd need to identify what we'd found."

"And did he think you found anything of significance?"

"Maybe," I answered. "We've mostly just found some random artifacts that seem to be from a variety of sources, but Levi found this large object that was so covered in sea crud that you couldn't even tell what it was. Once it was cleaned up a bit, we could see it was a large cross. Pono, the man who originally found the debris field, e-mailed a photo of it to Uncle Rory after he got back from diving yesterday, and Rory said he's almost certain the cross was part of a manifest from a ship called *The Isabella*."

"Sounds promising."

"Maybe. The thing is that Rory has papers that say *The Isabella* sank in 1802 in an area to the south of Hawaii known as the Kingman Reef."

"So it couldn't be from the same ship," Dad concluded.

"If the papers Rory has documenting the location of the shipwreck are accurate, then you're correct; the cross couldn't have come from *The Isabella* unless it was lost prior to the sinking of the ship. Still, the cross got Rory thinking. He has a theory that perhaps the cross was transferred to another ship in the fleet for some reason without the manifest having been updated. *The Isabella* was one of three merchant ships owned by the Santiago family, who sailed between South America and the Orient in the late eighteenth and early nineteenth centuries."

"Is the cross the only relic you found that seems to have belonged to this ship?"

"The only item we can specifically match. We also found a gold coin that's Spanish in origin, and a knife with a silver handle that has a mark that seems familiar but so far is unidentifiable. I found some English silverware, so at this point we don't know what, if anything, we have that's of value. We'll most likely be long gone before Pono and Malie figure out any of this, but it's been fun to go along for the ride, and the trip to the south shore yesterday was fun. Ellie and I even got to swim with turtles."

"I took a commercial dive boat to an area known as Turtle Town when I was on Maui a while back," Dad informed me.

"The place we snorkeled yesterday was really close to there. Malie works for an organization that tracks and protects the local sea turtle population. Ellie went to one of their organizational meetings while Zak, Levi, and I, were at the luau." I decided not to mention the murder so as not to worry my dad about things over which he had no control. "The program offers all sorts of volunteer opportunities. I might have to come back sometime when I have time to offer my help. By the way, how did the Events Committee meeting go yesterday?"

Levi, Ellie, and I are members of the Ashton Falls Events Committee, along with six other community members. It's the job of the committee to plan and execute the almost continuous series of celebrations and events that are sponsored by the town in an effort to bring the ever-important tourist dollar from the larger cities in the valley up the mountain to our little hamlet.

"It went well. It looks like everything is in place for the classic car event."

"I didn't get volunteered for anything, did I?" The event was set to take place the weekend after the gang and I returned, and I really didn't want to have to jump right into some huge commitment.

"Willa wanted to assign the snack bar to you, but I reminded her that there was no way you'd be ready, so Tawny agreed to oversee the food. It's been tough with you, Ellie, and Levi all gone at the same time, but I think those of us who remain have it covered."

"I've been thinking we really need to recruit some new members. With only nine of us, it seems like putting on these events is almost a full-time job."

"I agree. Let's bring it up at the next meeting," Dad said.

"Whatever happened with the location for the derby?" I asked. Part of the classic car event is a demolition derby that's normally held at the fairgrounds in Bryton Lake. But this year there's a scheduling conflict, and the Events Committee had been informed that we wouldn't be able to use that facility.

"Willa talked Old Man Johnson into letting us use the old corral out by his place. The fencing is falling down, but it can be made workable with some quick repairs, and the area is flat with little vegetation. One of the guys from the road crew is going to go out with a grader and get her ready."

"Good for Willa. How did she convince Johnson to let us use his property?"

Old Man Johnson was a nice-enough guy, but he was a total recluse who normally would shoot anyone who dared trespass on his property.

"Willa didn't go into any specifics, but I gathered that a large quantity of baked goods were involved in the negotiations."

I laughed. Johnson was known for his sweet tooth.

"I guess Jeremy warned you about letting your dogs run free."

"He called and spoke to your mother. Any word on the cause of all the animal deaths?"

"Not that I've heard," I answered. "I haven't spoken to Jeremy yet today, so he might have news."

"I noticed that he'd put up flyers around town, warning people to keep their animals restrained. Are you thinking we're dealing with poison?"

"I don't know. Maybe. It's the only thing that makes sense, but so far neither Jeremy nor Salinger have found any evidence of anything intentional. I'll keep you in the loop if I find out anything new."

"Have you checked the groundwater?" my dad asked.

"Groundwater?"

"It occurred to me that there's an underground spring in that marshy area near where the animal deaths have occurred. If something toxic got into the groundwater, it could have contaminated the spring."

"You think someone is dumping toxic chemicals in the area?" I asked.

"It's possible," Dad said. "It just occurred to me in the middle of the night when I was up walking Harper and Sophie wanted to go out. As I let her into the yard, I thought about Jeremy's warning and suddenly inspiration hit."

"The middle of the night is the best time for wonderful ideas," I agreed. "I'll call Salinger and have him test the water."

"I already did. I'll let you know what they find."

"Thanks. I hope you're right. Not that I hope the groundwater is contaminated, but the first step to containing the problem is to figure out the source. It looks like the tendency to play sleuth runs in the family."

Dad laughed. "Hardly. If Harper hadn't been fussy last night, the idea might never have come to me."

"How are Mom and Harper?" I asked. I realized that was an awkward segue, but I really wanted to broach the subject of my parents' living arrangements before my dad hung up.

"Both are fine. Harper seems to be having a hard time lately. I suspect she's getting her first tooth."

"Already? Isn't that early?" My baby sister was only two and a half months old.

"I guess these things happen at differing rates. It seems like you got your first tooth early as well."

"Mom mentioned that you moved back into the guesthouse," I said, deciding to jump right in.

"I thought it best."

"Best? How can it be best? Mom and Harper need you."

"I haven't gone anywhere," Dad assured me.

"You know what I mean. I talked to Mom, and I could tell she was upset. You have two children together; don't you think it's time to make a commitment?"

"I *do* think it's time for a commitment, which is why I asked your mother to marry me," Dad informed me.

If you could see me, you'd find that my jaw had dropped, and I'm sure I had a look of shock on my face.

"She said no?"

"She didn't say yes." My dad sighed. "She said she needed to think about things. I decided to move back to the guesthouse while she figures out what it is she really wants."

"Mom loves you."

"I know. I love her too."

"She just needs time to adjust to the idea."

"I've given her twenty-five years," my dad reminded me.

I had to admit Dad had a point. He'd been more than patient with Mom. Maybe it *was* time for Mom to figure out what it was she wanted.

"Don't give up on her," I pleaded.

After I hung up with my dad, I went in search of Ellie. She'd gone for another of her solitary walks, but I'd heard her come in while I was on the phone. I went into the living room and found her sitting cross-legged on the sofa. She was listening to what someone was saying on the other end of the phone she had plastered to her ear. She looked as shell-shocked as anyone I'd ever seen.

"Yes, I understand," she stammered.

In spite of the tan she'd obtained during our hours upon hours outdoors, Ellie looked as pale as a ghost.

"Yes, I'll do that. Thank you for letting me know."

Ellie hung up the phone and looked at me with hollow eyes.

"What is it?" I sat down next to her.

"That was my landlady. I'd told her that I would be moving out shortly after returning from my honeymoon, and apparently I forgot to tell her that my plans had changed."

"She rented the apartment," I gasped.

"She accepted a check for the first month's rent and a cleaning deposit today," Ellie confirmed.

"Did you explain what happened?"

"I did. She was sorry, but the couple came all the way from Tucson to look at the apartment. It seems they just got married and don't have a lot of money, so my very reasonably priced unit was a godsend."

"How long do you have?" I asked.

"I have to be out by the end of the month." Ellie put her forehead on her raised knees and began to weep.

I searched for the right thing to say. There are people in the world who are good at offering comfort and others who don't have a clue. I'm afraid that, more often than not, I fall into the latter category. I wanted to say something brilliant and comforting and absolutely perfect. If our roles were reversed, Ellie would know just what to do.

"I know this is difficult for you after everything you've already been through, but we'll find you something else," I jumped in. "There are other apartments in Ashton Falls. I'll help you look when we get back. Zak and Levi can help you move. Everything will be fine."

Ellie looked up at me, tear tracks on her cheeks. "I appreciate the pep talk, but my apartment was very affordable. Trust me when I tell you that there's nothing else in Ashton Falls even remotely close in rent."

"Ellie's Beach Hut is doing well. Maybe you can give yourself a raise."

"Truthfully, I'm barely hanging on. I know I've been busy, but making a profit in any type of restaurant is really hard. My business is seasonal; I've yet to establish a solid year-round clientele."

"Maybe your mom . . . ?"

"I'm not asking my mom to pay my rent," Ellie insisted.

"Yeah, I get that."

I'd had to ask my dad for financial help a couple of years ago and it had been one of the most humiliating things I'd ever done as an adult. He was very nice about it and seemed happy to help, but I'd felt like a child asking for an advance on her allowance.

"Listen, you can stay with me and Charlie until you figure this out," I offered.

"What about all my stuff?"

"We'll put it in storage. There are units at the bottom of the mountain in Bryton Lake. I've heard they're very affordable."

"You know how much I appreciate the offer, but your boathouse is little more than a studio. Where would I even sleep?"

I shrugged. "I have a big bed."

Ellie smiled. "A big bed with four occupants already, if you include Charlie and the cats. Five when Zak stays over."

"You can sleep on the sofa. Come on, El, it'll only be until we can find you something perfect."

Ellie appeared to be thinking about my offer. I knew she wanted to maintain her independence and not have to accept favors or rely on anyone, but rentals in Ashton Falls weren't cheap, and Ellie was correct in her assumption that finding something she could afford wouldn't be easy. I thought about the building Jeremy had lived in before Morgan was born, but I was pretty sure it didn't have any vacancies. Still, it wouldn't hurt to ask him about it when I spoke to him the next day. Jeremy had ended up getting a killer deal on a condo owned by our mutual friend, Phyllis King, who'd reduced his rent in exchange for getting the opportunity to babysit Jeremy's two-month-old daughter, Morgan Rose. I could ask Phyllis if any of the other condos in the complex were available, but chances were that without Phyllis's good-friend discount, the units would be much too expensive anyway.

"Okay," Ellie finally spoke, "but just for a couple of weeks, and only if I can't find anything before I have to move. I plan to start looking the minute we get home."

I smiled and gave Ellie a long, hard hug. Who knew the road back from her impulsive engagement would be such a difficult one?

Chapter 12

Ellie, Charlie, and I decided to walk down the street to the local farmers market, a festive affair where families from the area sold everything from produce to clothing and household items. Popular among both locals and tourists, the sidewalk was crowded with shoppers carrying large bags filled with their morning's find. I stopped to look at some tie-dyed skirts, really just long pieces of fabric that wrapped around your hips and tied at the side. They had both short and long versions that would be perfect to use as beach cover-ups.

"Let's get some more avocados," Ellie said. "I have a craving for some chips and guacamole."

"Those baked chips we got the last time were really good," I added. "I really wanted to try the onion/garlic flavor."

Ellie stopped to sort through the produce displayed on long tables under shade canopies. "The papaya look good, as do the pineapples and strawberries. Maybe a fruit salad for dinner?"

"Get some of the mangos too." I picked up a slice of the juicy fruit that had been left for shoppers to sample.

"How are we doing on tomatoes?" Ellie asked as I tasted a variety of freshly made spreads and salad dressings.

"We could probably use a few. What should we have for dinner? They still have a good selection of freshly caught fish."

"Fish sounds good. I thought I'd make some banana nut muffins with these macadamia nuts, and maybe a pineapple upside-down cake for dessert. The one we had at the restaurant was so good, I thought I'd try my hand at duplicating it."

My mouth began to water at the memory of the decadent cake.

"Do you think Pono and Malie will join us?" Ellie asked as she began to sort through giant ears of corn.

I shrugged. "I'm not sure, but it couldn't hurt to buy enough corn in case they decide to. I wonder how the hearing is going."

Ellie stopped what she was doing and turned to look at me. "Doesn't it seem just a tiny bit odd that Anton's partner got a new hearing in front of a new judge so soon after Anton was killed and the judge who made the original decision to grant the injunction went missing?"

"Actually, it seems very odd. And suspicious," I added. "In fact, I'd be willing to bet the injunction is behind both Anton's murder and Judge Gregor's disappearance. I'm just not exactly sure how. If we assume the murder is about getting the new hearing, then it seems odd that *any* judge would be privy to such a thing."

"Powerful people get bought all the time," Ellie reminded me.

"Yeah, I guess."

"Oh look, there's Luana from Makani's." Ellie waved at a woman with dark features who was sorting through a pile of lettuce. "I see you had the same idea we did," she said to the restaurant owner.

"I come four times a week to get fresh produce," Luana answered. She bent down to pet Charlie. "What a cute dog."

"His name is Charlie," I supplied.

"Can he have a cookie?" Luana asked. "It's macadamia nut."

"I'm sure he'd enjoy that," I answered. "Did you get the cookie here?"

"They're on the table next to the dips and dressings."

I looked back toward the table I'd just walked away from. "I'll have to get some before we leave. They look really good."

"They are. And while you're there, check out the pineapple salsa."

"I will. So far everything I've eaten here has been fabulous."

"There's a very talented group of hardworking people who make a living catering to those of us who prefer our food to be organic and locally grown." Luana picked up a slice of pineapple and tasted it. "Have you heard anything new about Anton's death?"

"Not really," I answered. "They released Pono, although I think he's still considered to be a person of interest. He doesn't seem overly concerned about the whole thing, so we pretty much decided to enjoy our vacation and let the police do their job."

"That's probably wise," Luana agreed.

"Look at these beautiful flowers," Ellie gushed as we made our way to the next booth, which was covered with flowers of every color in the rainbow.

"Kala, this is Ellie and Zoe," Luana introduced us to the woman selling the flowers. "Kala grows all of these in her garden."

"They're lovely." Ellie picked up a bunch of red hibiscus and took a deep breath of the intoxicating scent. "I'd love to have them, but I'm on a bit of a budget at the moment."

"I'm sure Kala would be willing to sell them to you for the price she charges the locals," Luana said.

"Certainly." Kala smiled as she suggested a very reasonable amount.

"Did you hear, they found the boat Brian and the others were last seen sailing away in?" Kala asked Luana after she had given Ellie her change.

"Really? Kala lives next door to Brian Boxer, one of the men who was sailing with Judge Gregor when his boat disappeared," Luana said, filling us in. She turned back to Kala. "You said they found the boat, but what about the men?"

"I'm afraid there was no sign of them. Poor Alana is a mess."

"Alana is Brian's wife," Luana explained. "They're having their first child in a few months."

"I'm so sorry," I said. "It must be horrible for her."

Kala nodded. "The not knowing is the worst."

"Have you heard what happened to the boat?" Luana asked.

"Alana said there was a large hole in the side, although there didn't appear to be anything in the area that it might have hit. The police suspect foul play since it sank about thirty miles north of where the men said they were going to be sailing. No one knows why the men were that far north. It's really a miracle they found the boat at all."

"Foul play?" My interest perked up. "Do they know what might have caused the hole?"

"No one knows," Kala answered. "The boat was in over two hundred feet of water. Divers swam down and confirmed that there were no bodies on board, but it's unlikely they'll know more until they can bring it up."

"I'm not much of a sailor," I commented, "but thirty miles seems to be quite a ways to be off course if you're only out for a pleasure cruise."

"It is," Kala confirmed, "especially because it was a calm day with only a gentle breeze, and all three men on board were experienced sailors. The location of the boat makes no sense at all. I'm afraid the consensus is that the men may have been attacked by pirates who they tried to outrun, only to lose in the end."

"Pirates?" Ellie said. "In this day and age?"

"Sure," Luana said. "There are still men who prey on the rich, although it doesn't make sense that they'd sink the boat. Normally, they kill the passengers but keep the boat."

By the time Ellie and I returned from the farmers market, the others had arrived. Zak and Levi were sharing a beer with Pono and Malie on the back patio. I helped Ellie put away the food we'd brought before opening my own beer and joining them.

"How was the surfing?" I asked.

"Awesome," Levi answered.

"And the hearing?" I turned to Pono and Malie.

"Anton's partner, Kingsley Portman, managed to talk Judge England into reviewing the injunction Judge Gregor had placed on the project." Pono sighed. "He is going to make a decision on Monday."

I frowned. "Does this whole thing seem a little too convenient to you?" I asked. "First Judge Gregor goes missing for no apparent reason, and then Anton's partner manages to get a new hearing in record time."

"You think Anton had something to do with Judge Gregor's disappearance?" Malie asked.

"Maybe." I explained what we'd discovered about the boat. "What if Anton sabotaged the boat so that he could bring the project in front of a new judge?"

"Okay, then who killed Anton?" Pono asked.

I had to stop to think about that. There were a lot of people who seemed to want Anton dead, and it was very possible that his death wasn't connected to the missing judge or the development, but if they *were* connected . . .

"What if Anton's partner is the one responsible for the judge going missing?" I offered. "Anton found out what Kingsley had done and made it known that he wasn't okay with what had happened, so Kingsley killed him."

"Kingsley wasn't on the island when Anton was murdered," Zak pointed out.

"So maybe Kingsley was working with someone who was at the party," I reasoned.

Malie frowned. "I don't know. It seems like a long shot. If someone wanted Judge Gregor dead, why not just break into his house and kill him, or jump him as he walked to his car? Why go to all the trouble of sinking a boat with three men on board?"

"What if whoever sank the boat wanted all three men dead?" I postulated. "If each man had been killed separately, there would be an obvious connection that the police would easily identify. Maybe the killer felt that connection could lead the police back to him. But if a boat sinks during a recreational cruise and all three men aboard happen to die, people would look at it quite differently."

"Zoe has a point." Ellie sat forward. "We spoke to Luana and a woman selling flowers at the market named Kala. There was a suggestion that pirates could be responsible for the fate of the boat."

"Pirates don't normally sink the boat they steal," Pono said.

"True, but I think the fact that pirates are being discussed makes a point. If the men had all been gunned down in their homes or offices, we'd be trying to identify their common enemies."

"Okay, so say that someone *did* want all three men dead. Why?" I asked.

"Gregor probably made many enemies as a judge," Pono pointed out. "Brian Boxer is an environmental attorney and Trenton Baldwin a developer. It's possible the three men were working on a project that might have posed a threat to Anton and his partner."

Malie bit her thumbnail as she appeared to consider Pono's theory. "I don't know. I realize that Anton wasn't popular among a certain segment of the population, but I don't buy the fact that he'd kill three men over money. There has to be something more going on. Anton could be ruthless, but I can't believe he was a killer."

"And Kingsley Portman?" I asked.

"I don't know him all that well," Malie said. "Anton knew how I felt about the development of our sensitive lands and made a point of not talking business with me when we were dating."

"I still can't believe you dated that guy," Pono complained.

"Yes, well, what about Sheila?" Malie shot back.

"Sheila never killed anyone."

"That you know of."

"So back to the missing men . . ." I said. I had no idea who Sheila was, but I assumed it was someone Pono dated of whom Malie didn't approve. It was easy to see there was tension between the two friends where certain subjects were concerned. "Is there a way we can find out what Brian and Trenton were working on? If we can find a link between the attorney and the developer, maybe we can link it to the judge as well. It could point us in a direction."

"I thought we were going to leave Anton's death to the cops so we could focus on the treasure hunt," Levi said.

"Yeah, we did say that," I admitted. I thought about Brian's pregnant wife; even though I'd never met her, I had a strong desire to help find the answers that would give her a small amount of peace. Not knowing what had happened to the man you loved must be the worst.

"I know Brian's assistant, Rebecca," Malie offered. "I can call to have a chat with her. Maybe in light of everything that's happened, she will be willing to discuss the matter."

"It's too late to dive today, but I say we go ahead and go tomorrow as planned," Pono said. "I have a feeling deep in my gut that we're right on the brink of finding something."

"I'd like to go diving," Levi agreed.

"Zoe?" Zak asked me.

"I'd like to hear what Malie comes up with, but unless it's something concrete that we can act on, I'm good with diving as well."

"I'll go inside and call Rebecca right now to see what I can find out."

I watched Malie get up and walk across the patio toward the open wall of the living area.

"I'm going to go in to grab another beer." Zak stood. "Anyone else?"

"I'll take one," Pono decided.

"Anyone else?"

"I'm getting hot," Ellie announced. "I think I'll go for a swim."

"I'll go with you," Levi offered as Ellie pulled off the shorts she'd put on over her swimsuit.

"Last one in is a rotten egg," Ellie challenged as she took off running toward the surf, Levi following close behind. By the time they'd made it to the waves, they were frolicking like puppies as each tried to gain the upper hand over the other in some sort of imaginary contest.

"So Levi and Ellie . . ." Pono said as he watched them play. "Are they a couple?"

Talk about a loaded question. I decided on the easy answer. "Just friends."

"Malie and I have been friends since we were toddlers," Pono shared. "Our mothers were friends."

"Levi, Ellie, and I all sat at the same table in kindergarten and have been best friends ever since."

"Ah, but now you have Zak," Pono pointed out.

I smiled.

"It changes the dynamic," Pono put forth.

I thought about that for a moment. "Yeah, I guess it does."

Ellie screeched with laughter as she jumped onto Levi's back and tried to dunk him under the surface of the water. It did my heart good to see her smile after the rough start she'd had on the trip. I thought about Pono's observation about Zak's entering our lives effecting the overall equilibrium of the best-friend triad. I hadn't realized it, but I could see that he had a point. The dynamic *had* changed. My relationship with Zak had created a separation of sorts between myself and Levi and Ellie. I certainly didn't spend as much time with them as I once had. Additionally, with the introduction of Zak, our threesome had become a foursome, creating a situation in which Levi and Ellie could feel free to pursue a romantic relationship without worrying that I'd end up feeling like a third wheel. I knew they had feelings for each other, and while the thought of a romance between the two of them had sent me into convulsions initially, I could see how a pairing might very well be the ultimate outcome.

A future in which Levi and Ellie married and raised a family left me with a much warmer feeling than one in which Ellie gave birth to a baby conceived from the donation of some random guy. Of course, they had obstacles to overcome. Many, many obstacles, the greatest of them being that in many ways Levi was still a child himself.

Zak returned to the patio and handed Pono the beer he'd requested. Charlie had wandered into the shade and was fast asleep. The men entered into a conversation about fishing that I intentionally tuned out. I felt my mind drifting as I watched Levi and Ellie playing in the waves. Our two-week stay in Maui was half over. Where had the time gone?

"Did you get through to Rebecca?" Pono asked.

"I did." Malie took a sip of Pono's beer and then settled into the lounge chair beside his. "She said that as far as she knew, the three men were not working on anything together. She had noticed that Brain had been uptight lately, and the men decided to go for a sail to forget their problems for a few hours. If there was more to the trip than that, she wasn't privy to it."

"So we go diving?" Pono asked. "I'm free tomorrow and Friday."

"I'm good with tomorrow, but as for Friday . . ." Malie hesitated. "Rebecca told me that a memorial service for Anton is going to be combined with Keoke's annual Fourth of July party, which will be held on Friday at Keoke's house on Oahu. It seems there was an announcement in the newspaper. Anton's family is having his body flown back to his hometown for burial, but Keoke is planning a service in Hawaii for anyone who would like to attend."

"So?" Pono shrugged.

"He was your sister's fiancé. Don't you think you should go?"

"My sister thinks I killed Anton. Why would she want me there?"

"Leia doesn't think you killed Anton," Malie argued.

"If Leia wanted me at the service, she would have called to ask me to attend. She didn't."

Malie took Pono's hand in hers and looked him in the eye. "I doubt Leia has the presence of mind to personally call anyone right now," she pointed out. "I'm sure she's expecting you to be there. You are her brother. It's what families do."

"Come with me," Pono persuaded.

"I really shouldn't."

"I'm not going alone."

"Zoe, Ellie, Levi, and I have been invited to Keoke's party. Perhaps we should all go together," Zak suggested.

Chapter 13

Thursday, July 3

Although the sand was warm, the air had cooled as a blanket of dark clouds passed overhead. I pulled my long, curly hair into a sloppy topknot as I settled onto a beach towel with my sandwich. Pono, Malie, Levi, and I had spent the morning in the water, gathering artifacts from the ocean floor. Ellie, who'd waited in the boat with Charlie, had sorted and stored everything. I felt like we'd had a successful morning in spite of the fact that my muscles ached and my hair might never recover from all the saltwater it had been exposed to this past week.

"Looks like a storm is coming," Ellie commented as she nibbled on a fresh strawberry as big as her fist.

Afternoon rain wasn't uncommon on the islands, but the particular clouds that gathered overhead looked more ominous than usual.

"I suppose we should head in after we eat," Pono said reluctantly.

The breeze picked up as the sky darkened. I rubbed my hands over my arms for warmth. The temperature most likely was still in the seventies, but my hair and swimsuit were both wet, causing a chill as the sun disappeared behind the cloud cover.

"Take my sweatshirt." Zak unzipped the sweatshirt he'd tossed on over his bare chest when we'd docked on the island. He wrapped it around my shoulders.

"Won't you be cold?" I couldn't help but admire Zak's well-defined chest, which had been bronzed by the sun.

"I'm fine. These sandwiches are really good. What kind of fish did you use?"

"Ono," Malie answered. "Try the macadamia nut spread with the strawberries. It's a really interesting combination."

"Do you think we found anything significant this morning?" I asked as I added a slice of avocado to my sandwich. We'd gotten an early start and had already completed two dives, each one resulting in several artifacts found, including a necklace that appeared to be worth quite a lot of money.

"The necklace looks like the one in this photo." Malie wiped her hands on a napkin, then picked up a sheet of paper and passed it to me.

After Rory identified the cross Zak had found on the previous trip as belonging to *The Isabella*, he'd copied and forwarded the ship's manifest as well as photos of some of the items to Malie. I have to admit there is a certain rush to be had from searching for treasure that has been resting on the bottom of the sea for hundreds of years.

"Is this enough to positively identify the ship we're looking for as *The Isabella*?" Levi asked as he peered over my shoulder.

"I'm not sure." Malie took a bite of her sandwich and then set it aside. She dug into her bag for the stack of documents she had copied and brought with her. "Several of the artifacts we've found seem to be from her manifest, but the information found in Rory's books indicate that *The Isabella* sank off the Kingman Reef, so something isn't lining up."

"Maybe that isn't where she sank after all," Pono postulated. "Maybe the information in the books is incorrect. It happens."

"No, *The Isabella* was found and excavated by a treasure hunter in 1926. See, there are pictures of some of the items recovered from the wreck." Malie passed the photos to Pono. "The only theory I can come up with is that a portion of the items listed on her manifest was transferred to another ship prior to sailing, but the paperwork was never updated. The family who owned *The Isabella* owned two other merchant ships, *The Maria* and *The Sofia*. Based on the research Rory has managed to complete in the past couple of days, *The Maria* was retired in 1887, so my guess is that we are looking for *The Sofia*."

"What if the cargo wasn't moved?" I asked. "What if the items we've found were sold to or stolen by the captain or crew of whatever ship sank in this area? Maybe the cross and the necklace were on *The Isabella* at one point but were removed prior to her run-in with the reef. You mentioned that she made stops at several ports along the west coast of the Americas before making her final journey across the Pacific Ocean."

I grabbed the stack of napkins as the wind threatened to send them across the sand.

"That's a good point," Malie realized. "I suppose that if the items were stolen, the captain of *The Isabella* might not even have been aware they were missing, which could be why the manifest was never altered. A theft could also explain why we have found items from many different ships. What if there was someone who stole items from all the ships in a port and then set off on his own? If the ship later sank with the ill-gotten gains, the treasure would have originated in several different places."

"Okay, so if we aren't looking for *The Isabella* or *The Sofia*, what ship are we looking for?" Levi asked.

"I'm not sure there is any way to know." Malie sighed.

"We'll figure it out." Pono laid an arm over her shoulder in a show of comfort and support.

"What if there isn't a ship?" Ellie asked as she brushed sand off her leg and adjusted her position on the blanket we'd brought from the house. "Isn't it possible there are situations that could cause specific items to end up on the ocean floor other than a shipwreck?"

"Such as?" Levi asked.

"Pirates," Ellie suggested. "Maybe *The Isabella* was robbed and the pirates who stole the cargo were careless and some of it fell overboard during a storm."

"Seems kind of unlikely," I pointed out.

"But possible," Ellie insisted.

I shrugged. "Yeah, I guess it's possible."

"Winds really kicking up," Zak commented.

"Guess we're in for a quick trip home." Pono seemed unaffected by the dramatic change in the weather.

"And a rocky one." Ellie groaned as she looked out toward the surf, which was becoming rougher by the minute.

"What are we going to do if we actually find a ship?" Malie asked as she began gathering the food and storing it in the basket she'd brought. "We don't have the equipment or money to orchestrate a full-on salvage operation."

Pono looked at Zak. "I suppose if we do find a ship and are able to positively identify her, we'll have to look for backers to fund the salvage operation."

Zak shrugged. "Let's find the ship and then we can discuss the next step. How much do you think the items we've found so far are worth even if we don't find the bulk of the cargo?"

Malie, who was kneeling on the blanket, leaned back on her heels and picked up the necklace. It was a heavy gold chain with a lacy gold design shaped like a tree, each of the branches of which held a gem of a different type. My guess was that it was some sort of mother's necklace, each stone representing a person in a family tree.

"I'm no jeweler," she said, "but I'd be willing to bet this one item is worth more than I make in a year."

"Hello, new boat." Pono grinned.

"We can't sell it," Malie informed him. "At least not yet. We should keep everything we find close to the vest until we figure out what, if anything, all of this might lead to. But it is pretty awesome."

"It's really pretty," I acknowledged. "And heavy. Do you think someone actually wore this?"

"Probably not." Pono took the necklace from Malie. "What do those papers tell you about what else we can expect to find?"

"It depends." Malie paused. "If we're operating under the assumption that part of the cargo of *The Isabella* somehow ended up here rather than where she went down, I guess we can compare the original manifest with the inventory of artifacts found to see what is missing. If we're operating under the assumption that some of the cargo from *The Isabella* was moved to another ship, I suppose we can expect to find those items plus the original cargo of the ship that actually went down in this area and any other items purchased or stolen from other ships, if that is indeed what occurred."

"I guess we keep diving," Pono said.

"I guess we do." Malie smiled. "But not today. We really should get going."

Everyone got up and began gathering the items we'd brought to the beach.

"Charlie," I called.

He didn't appear.

"Charlie," I called louder.

Still no dog.

"I'll go look for him," Zak offered.

"I'll go with you."

I tried to run to keep up with Zak, but his sweatshirt, which hung past my knees, was getting in the way, so I took it off and wrapped it around my waist.

"Charlie," I yelled as loud as I could.

The wind was whistling and waves were crashing, creating a loud background noise that drowned out my shouts. I knew in the back of my mind that we were on an island and Charlie couldn't have gone far, but it was unlike him to simply wander off, so I couldn't help but feel the first stirrings of panic. With each minute we searched and were unable to find him, my anxiety grew.

"Don't worry; he's around here somewhere," Zak assured me.

"I know. It's just not like him to take off like this."

Actually, it was exactly like him to take off like this, but only when . . . I didn't want to think about that.

I stood still and turned slowly in a circle, looking carefully for any sign of my furry best friend. The wind blew my hair from the topknot I'd hastily created, making it all but impossible to keep it out of my face.

"Maybe we should split up," Zak said. "You head to the right and I'll go left. Meet me back here in this exact spot in twenty minutes, whether you've found him or not."

"Okay." I kissed Zak and then headed toward sand dunes that had created a sandstorm in the wind. If anything had happened to Charlie, I'd never forgive myself. I should have been watching him more closely. How could I have let him wander off? He must have become disoriented with all the sand. I prayed he wasn't hurt or frightened.

"Charlie," I continued to call as I struggled against the wind. Tears streamed down my face, mixing with the blowing sand to make a sort of mudpack. I knew I must look like a mess, but I didn't care. All I cared about was finding Charlie.

It had been over ten minutes. I'd need to turn back if I was going to keep to the timeline Zak and I had set up. I paused to consider my next move when I heard Charlie barking in the distance.

"Charlie," I called as I ran toward the sound.

He continued to bark, but it didn't appear he was coming toward me. Visions of his broken and bloody body raced through my mind as I ran as fast as I could in the blowing, sifting sand. As I made my way toward the sound of his barking, I saw Charlie standing next to what looked to be a bunker of some type. I remembered Rory saying that the island had been used by the military in the past. I called to Charlie, but he continued to pace in front of the structure, barking all the while.

I closed the distance between us in record time. I dropped to my knees and hugged Charlie to my chest. "Why did you run off?" I sobbed. "You scared the heck out of me."

Charlie licked my face as if in apology for causing me so much stress. I picked him up and was turning to get back to the spot where I was to meet Zak when Charlie wiggled out of my arms and returned to the entrance of the underground bunker.

"Charlie, it's empty," I said, trying to reason with my frantic little dog. "It has been for a long time."

Charlie continued to pace and bark.

"Zak is waiting for us. We need to go," I insisted.

Charlie began jumping against the door, which was locked with a fairly new padlock. I frowned, and for the first time since I'd found him, I really looked around. There were footprints. A lot of them. The blowing sand had buried many of the prints leading to the structure, but the area behind it was protected by the wind. I also noticed that there were cigarette butts littering the ground that looked to be fresh. Someone had been here recently.

"Did you see someone?" I asked Charlie.

He jumped against the door and began scratching, as if trying to get in.

"Did someone go inside?"

Charlie sat down and looked at me. I knew he was trying to work out a way to tell me whatever it was he wanted me to understand. I tried the lock, but it was secure. The door didn't give at all, and the bunker didn't have any windows. The structure was only raised several feet above the ground. It was covered with sand and shrubbery so as not to be seen from the air. I'd seen similar structures on military bases. Most times they were used to store ammo.

I was debating what to do when Zak walked up behind me. "Thank God you found him."

"There's something in that bunker that Charlie wants us to find," I told Zak. "Every time I try to leave, he throws a fit and starts scratching at the door."

Zak frowned. He tried the lock, as I had. He motioned for me to be silent as he put his ear against the door. "I hear banging."

"What kind of banging?" I asked.

"I think its Morse Code." Zak continued to listen. "It's definitely an SOS. We need to get this door open. Someone is locked inside."

I looked around. We didn't have any tools. "How are we going to break the lock?"

"I'm sure there must be something on the boat."

"I'll stay with Charlie while you go. Bring the others. We might need help."

Zak probably wasn't gone all that long, but it seemed like forever. The island, which had once been inhabited, was now deserted, creating a ghost town. I stopped for the first time to look around at the deserted buildings in the distance. I noticed a sign warning people to stay away because there were likely to be unexploded shells in the area. I thought about my mad dash across the island. It was a good thing I hadn't stumbled across any of the live shells the sign warned of. The island had been used for combat training and as a bombing target. It made sense that bombs might have been dropped that for whatever reason had failed to detonate and remained hidden as live ammo.

Suddenly, the stress I'd been feeling left my body and I realized I was exhausted. I sank to the ground and wrapped my arms around Charlie, who seemed more than happy to cuddle now that he was satisfied I wasn't going to leave. It didn't make any sense that there would be a person or persons inside the bunker. The door was locked from the outside. Who would lock someone in such a desolate location?

I watched as Zak returned with an armful of tools, as well as the other members of our party. Ellie and I stood back while Zak, Levi, Pono, and Malie discussed what to do. Normally, I'd want to be in on the discussion, but I found that my brain had settled into a state of numbness. After several minutes and at least ten attempts to break the lock, the door was finally opened. Zak, Levi, and Pono went inside, while Malie held the door open to provide light. When the men returned, they had three additional people with them.

"Judge Gregor!" Malie helped the man to a spot away from the bunker that had been his prison. "Are you all right?"

"I'm fine. We all are. It's just taking a bit of time for my eyes to adjust to the light."

The other two men, who I assumed were Brian Boxer and Trenton Baldwin, had been helped to a spot next to the judge.

"We need to get back and call the police," Pono said.

"No," Gregor commanded.

Chapter 14

By the time we got home, it was late into the evening. Talk about a crazy day. Judge Gregor had insisted that we not notify the police until we could talk things out and come up with a plan. Lives, he insisted, other than theirs, were still in danger. News of their rescue could trigger a situation that would lead to the deaths of other captives.

"Here's your wine." Zak handed me a glass. Ellie had opted to go to bed and Levi was inside, watching television. Zak and I sat on the patio overlooking the ocean. The storm had blown in and created a rough, wet ride home, but as with most tropical storms, it had blown out within a matter of hours.

Zak and I sat side by side in silence, each lost in our own thoughts as we watched the waves rhythmically roll into shore. Charlie was snoring from the bottom of my chair and once again all felt right with the world. I thought about everything we'd learned today, all the pieces to the puzzle that had seemed to fall into place. And all the other pieces that still didn't fit at all.

It turned out that Judge Gregor, Brian Boxer, and Trenton Baldwin had gone sailing after receiving an invitation to meet up with some men who belonged to the same yacht club they did. When they arrived at the marina, they were given a note that said that the others couldn't make it, but they should go anyway, which they did. In retrospect, the men realized that the invitation must have been forged by whoever wanted them to go sailing that day.

While sailing to the north of Maui, they came across a boat that was still, appearing to be in distress. When they pulled up to see if they could lend a hand, there were men wearing masks onboard. They had guns and quickly boarded Judge Gregor's boat. After tying Gregor and the others up, the masked men forced them onto their vessel and sailed farther to the north after sinking the judge's yacht. Then the masked men brought them to the island and locked them in the bunker.

They were left with food and water that lasted three days, after which the masked gunmen came back and left more supplies. The pattern had been repeated every few days for as long as the men had been held captive. Gregor reported that the men never spoke or removed their masks, so they had no way of identifying who they might be or why they had been kidnapped.

On one of the supply runs, the captives overheard one of the masked men talking about other people being held in some other location. It sounded as if once a decision of some sort was made, all of them would be dealt with.

Judge Gregor's opinion was that the kidnapping had taken place as a result of his ruling on the resort project. It seemed crazy to me that anyone would go to all that trouble over a simple project, but the judge pointed out that the profit to be made would be hundreds of millions of dollars. All three men in the bunker were involved in the injunction in one way or the other, and it made sense that for the injunction to be overturned, all of them would need to be out of the way.

Judge Gregor had ruled on the injunction. The likelihood of arranging a hearing with a different judge who might rule differently on it while Gregor was still in the mix was slim.

Brian Boxer had been the attorney for the conservation group that had sponsored the campaign to get the injunction issued in the first place.

Trenton Baldwin, a developer himself, had provided studies he'd requisitioned when he'd considered building on the same exact spot years earlier. After the environmental impact reports had come back, he'd decided to move on to another location. He believed that the work he'd done in the past was what had led to the current injunction.

It was the belief of the three men that they had been kept alive to be used as a bargaining chip to ensure that the injunction would be overturned.

"What do you think will happen on Monday?" I asked Zak.

"I suppose that after all of the trouble the kidnappers have gone to, they must be fairly certain the new judge will overturn the injunction."

"Do you think the kidnappers planned to kill the captives either way?"

Zak considered that. "Perhaps not. The kidnappers have gone to a lot of effort both to keep the men alive and to conceal their own identities. There's a chance they would have let them go after the decision was made."

"But it would be cleaner to kill them and let the world think they drowned in the boat accident," I pointed out.

"True. I suppose that if word got out about what actually happened to the men, a new decision on the injunction would be looked at closely. Gregor can't prove that the reason the men were kidnapped is because of the project, but it does seem likely, and they probably wouldn't have a hard time creating suspicion even if they couldn't actually prove anything."

"It seems Kingsley Portman has to be involved in this," I asserted.

"I agree."

I took a sip of my wine and considered things. The men we'd rescued insisted that if word of their rescue was made public, it would put the other captives in danger, so we'd taken them to a secure location where they could be reunited with their families without anyone knowing they'd been found. Judge Gregor insisted that we contact one man and one man only on the local police force. It was his opinion that there might be one or more dirty cops involved in the setup.

The three men we rescued said that when the kidnappers had dropped off supplies that morning, they'd mentioned that they wouldn't be back until Monday, after the decision was made public. We all hoped that was true, which would mean that the kidnappers wouldn't know the men had been freed until the other captives could be identified and located.

"Are we still planning to make the trip to Oahu tomorrow?" I asked.

"We did tell Keoke we would attend his party, and he's been more than gracious."

"Yeah, I guess we should go." I was quiet for a moment. "Brian mentioned that one of the kidnappers had a tattoo on the inside of his wrist. Keoke has a tattoo on the inside of his wrist."

"You think he's one of the kidnappers?" Zak sounded shocked by my suggestion.

"Anton did die at Keoke's party," I pointed out. "And let's not forget that Keoke makes his money investing in projects much like Anton's. Maybe the potential loss of hundreds of millions of dollars was enough to cause him to act in a way he wouldn't have otherwise."

I had to give Zak credit. He did take a moment to stop to think about what I had said before answering. "No," he eventually decided. "Keoke wouldn't kidnap anyone, and he certainly wouldn't kill Anton."

I wasn't as sure as Zak but decided to let it go for the moment. It was such a beautiful night; a night for romance rather than murder, kidnapping, and conspiracy. I'd made the decision several nights earlier to bring more romance into the mix, but somehow, in spite of my resolve, Zak and I had barely managed to spend any time together. I realized that the trip was a group trip and as such we'd be involved in group activities. Still, I guess I thought we'd have *some* time to ourselves.

"It feels like a nice night for a swim," I said.

Zak looked at the pool and arched an eyebrow.

"Not the pool," I clarified.

"Haven't you had enough saltwater today?"

I got up from my chair and pulled Zak to his feet. Charlie looked at us and then decided to go back to sleep. I stood on tiptoe and pulled Zak's shirt over his head.

"The waves are gentle, the moon is full, Ellie is sleeping, Levi is occupied," I whispered suggestively as I kissed Zak's neck.

"I like where you're going with this." Zak groaned. "Do you have your swimsuit on?"

I pulled my shirt over my head. "Don't need one."

Chapter 15

Friday, July 4

"How's my snuggle baby?" I asked.

"Harper is fine," my dad said. "Although she misses her big sister. How is the trip?"

"Fun. We're flying to Oahu to attend a Fourth of July celebration at Zak's friend's house today. I hear he has a spectacular estate right on the water."

"Sounds like fun."

"Yeah, it's supposedly *the* party to attend. I guess he goes all out with caterers and a fireworks display over the water. I'm really looking forward to it, although I'll miss the annual Ashton Falls event. Are you going to take my baby sister to see the fireworks?"

"They don't start until almost ten," Dad pointed out.

"So?"

"Harper is two months old. Ten o'clock is just a tad past her bedtime. I think your mom and I are going to take her to the potluck picnic in the park. Jeremy is bringing Morgan, so they can have a playdate."

"Oh," I moaned. "I'm going to miss it."

"I doubt the babies will be doing a lot of playing."

"I know, but it's Harper's first Fourth. Is she wearing the outfit I bought her?"

"Does it have red and blue stars on a white background?"

"That's the one."

"Then yes, that's what her mother dressed her in."

"Take a picture of her and text it to me."

"I'm not at the house at the moment. I thought I'd take the dogs for a nice long walk before we leave, but I'll take the photo when I get back," Dad promised.

"That would be fine. Any word on the water Salinger had tested?" I asked.

"Actually, yes," Dad said. "They found significant amounts of several toxic chemicals, which led Salinger to conclude that the water was contaminated with waste created by the cooking of methamphetamine. They've enclosed the swamp area I mentioned until they can get it cleaned up, so hopefully we won't have any more animal fatalities."

"Wow, I'm really glad to hear that. Did they find out who was doing the dumping?"

"Not yet, but they're looking into a couple of leads."

"I'm surprised Jeremy didn't call me."

"He said he tried, but his calls went straight to voice mail."

I took out my phone and looked at it. I had seven missed calls. "I went diving yesterday and I guess I forgot to check my messages when I got back into range. It was a really long day."

"Did you find additional artifacts?" Dad asked.

"Better. We found three men in a bunker."

I spent the next several minutes filling him in on everything that had happened, after making him swear that he wouldn't tell anyone. Not that the average citizen of Ashton Falls would have cause to spread the word of the men's rescue to Maui, but the disappearance of the judge had made the national news, so you never knew who might say what to whom.

"Sounds like you might have gotten yourself mixed up with some pretty dangerous people. Best be careful who you talk to," Dad warned.

"I'm sure we'll be perfectly safe at Keoke's party. We fly home on Wednesday, so we only have half a week next week. I really miss everyone and am anxious to get home, but I'm disappointed we haven't found the shipwreck yet."

"Finding the actual ship, if there even is one, could take years," Dad pointed out.

"I know. It's been really fun looking, though."

"Is Ellie doing better" Dad asked.

"She is, although she forgot to notify her landlady that she wasn't going to move after all and her apartment has been rented. She has to move out by the end of the month, so keep an eye out for a new place she can afford."

"I'll ask around. I'm sure we can find her something."

After I hung up, I went in search of the others. Levi and Ellie were deep in conversation on the patio. I hated to disturb them and was about to retreat back into the house when Ellie noticed me and waved me over. I couldn't help but notice the slight blush on

Ellie's cheeks. I would be willing to bet I'd interrupted a personal conversation of the intimate kind.

"Levi and I are thinking about skipping the Oahu trip," Ellie informed me. "I really hoped to make the trip around the island to Hana, but with all the diving I haven't had the opportunity. Levi said he'd be happy to stay behind and go with me."

"That's fine." I smiled. I suspected there was more to the decision to remain on Maui than a sightseeing trip but didn't say as much. "The party at Keoke's will be fun, but you guys won't really know a lot of people."

"We'll keep Charlie with us, if you'd like," Levi offered. "I'm sure he'd like the quiet drive and a nice long hike in the rain forest more than a day on a leash at a stranger's house."

"We plan to stay overnight," I reminded my friends.

"That's fine. Charlie can sleep with me tonight," Ellie said.

I thought about the offer. I had been a little worried about how Charlie would fare with an estate full of strangers. Leaving him with Levi and Ellie seemed a perfect solution.

"Okay, thanks," I agreed. "I read an article about the road to Hana in one of the travel magazines in the living room. It seems like there are a lot of really good hikes along the way, so you should probably get started. It takes a lot longer to make the trip than the mileage would suggest."

"I was just going in to grab my stuff," Ellie informed me.

"Have you seen Zak?" I asked Levi.

"He was out here with us but got a call and headed back toward the house. He's probably in the bedroom."

"Have fun today."

I managed to catch the end of Zak's conversation. Based on the little bit I overheard, it sounded as though Zak was speaking to the police detective Judge Gregor had asked us to call the previous day. The fact that I'd found the men and there were six of us who were present when the police arrived to escort them to the secure location, yet it was Zak who was called with an update brought home what I thought was an important fact: although Zak, Levi, Ellie, and I were all the same age, it was Zak everyone considered to be the adult. Perhaps it was because he had a *lot* more money than the rest of us, or more worldly experience, but I suspected it was due more to the way he handled himself in a variety of situations.

"Anything new?" I asked after he hung up.

"The men have all been reunited with their families, and a select group of local law-enforcement officials have been recruited to quietly investigate. As of now, they still don't know who's responsible for the kidnapping or where the other captives are being held. I did find it interesting that there were no recent missing persons reports."

"So if there are others, they're people who haven't been missed."

"Perhaps. Or it could be that the families of the captives have been warned not to notify the police."

"Has anyone thought to question Kingsley Portman?" I asked.

"They purposely haven't spoken with him. If he is involved, they don't want him to realize that the judge and the others have been found. I think that once they can locate the others and make sure they're safe, he'll be the first one they talk to."

"I guess I can see that making sure everyone is unharmed and accounted for is their top priority. One way or the other, everything is going to come to a head when the new judge rules on Monday. I know you don't want to believe that Keoke is involved, but . . ."

"A lot of men have tattoos on their wrists," Zak pointed out.

"I suppose, but . . ."

"Zoe, please. You just have to trust me on this; Keoke isn't involved in Judge Gregor's kidnapping or Anton's murder."

I decided not to argue with Zak. I would, after all, be a guest in Keoke's home for twenty-four hours. Perhaps I'd take that opportunity to look around.

Chapter 16

Zak and I took an early flight to the island and then rented a car. By the time we arrived at the estate, Pono and Malie were already in attendance. I was glad they'd decided to come. Both communicated that they only planned to stay for a short while, but I was still glad to see familiar faces in an unfamiliar crowd. I chatted with Malie while Zak greeted Pono, who was speaking to a man I didn't recognize.

"I love your dress," I complimented Malie, who wore a traditional Hawaiian outfit with an orange and brown print. The colors in the dress flattered her dark hair and skin. She'd tucked an orange flower over one ear, rounding out the ensemble.

"Thank you. I wear this same dress to this party every year, but I really love it. Your outfit is nice as well."

I wore a simple white sundress that really wasn't anything special except for its tendency to travel without wrinkling, so I didn't respond to Malie's polite yet I suspected insincere comment. "I wasn't expecting such a large crowd. It looks like half the people who live on the island must be here today."

Malie laughed. "You're closer to the truth than you think. Keoke likes to do it up big, so he invites everyone he knows, as well as everyone they know. He often places announcements in the local paper, inviting the general populace, as well."

I looked at the long buffet tables, which had been set up under canopies to protect the food from the hot sun. The tables were overflowing with fresh fruits and vegetables, salads, a variety of fish, seafood, sushi, and traditional Hawaiian dishes such as poi and rice.

"It must cost a fortune to feed all these people," I said, and my mouth began to water when I noticed the table set off to the side overloaded with a variety of delicious-looking desserts. If I wasn't mistaken, both cream puffs and cheesecake, two of my favorites, were set out on platforms that were arranged over trays of ice that chilled the perishables.

Malie shrugged. "Keoke is a wealthy man. He enjoys entertaining and does so often. I'm pretty sure he could launch a successful bid for governor if he wanted to."

"Do you think he's interested in politics?"

"I guess you could say he's not *uninterested*, although he hasn't thrown his hat in the ring quite yet. His business keeps him busy, although I heard he was looking to take on a partner so he can devote more time to other interests. Who knows? Maybe he's feeling out the idea."

A bid for governor would surely be a huge undertaking, but Keoke had wealth, good looks, and—based on the number of people in attendance—a lot of friends.

"Have you known Keoke long?"

"Most of my life. Pono and I have been best friends since we were in diapers, and Leia and I have always been close as well, although things got pretty awkward once Anton dumped me for her."

"How long ago was that?"

"Three months."

"Really?" I was surprised. Leia and Anton had been engaged to be married. I guess I assumed they had been dating for quite some time. Poor Malie. It was no wonder she felt awkward socializing with Leia. The wounds were still fresh.

"Three really long months," Malie emphasized. "Now that I've had time to gain perspective, I can see that Anton and I might not have been right for each other, but it really stung that Leia would be so callous when it came to my feelings. I'm not sure if Leia and I can ever return to the friendship we once shared."

"I can imagine. I hadn't known everything had happened so recently. I apologize for not realizing how much Anton's death must have affected you as well."

Malie wiped away a tear. I could see she was deeply affected by everything that had happened in spite of the fact that she fought to appear unaffected. "That's okay. Sometimes I look back and wonder how things would have turned out if I hadn't taken Anton to Keoke's party. Part of me thinks Anton and I would still be together, but then, if I am honest with myself, I'm pretty sure the only reason he asked me out in the first place was because Kingsley convinced him that it might make a difference in my actions regarding the project we were arguing over."

"Did it?" I had to ask.

"No, not really. Although I suppose I might have been more willing to listen to Anton's side of things, so maybe Kingsley was right after all."

"Is Kingsley here today?" I wondered.

"I saw him earlier." Malie looked around as she attempted to find the man in the crowd. "See the man in the black coat?"

I turned toward a group of men, one of whom I recognized as Jeffrey, Anton's best man. I'd met him briefly at the luau. He was talking to a short but elegantly dressed man who looked to be of Japanese descent.

"You mean the man talking to Jeffrey?" I asked.

"I never met Jeffrey," Malie said, "but if he is the tall man in the black shirt, then yes. The short man with him is Kingsley."

I frowned. "He looks Japanese. Kingsley Portman isn't much of a Japanese name."

"His mom is Japanese and his dad is Caucasian. I think his father was from England originally. Kingsley grew up in Japan."

"I didn't realize you'd never met Jeffrey. He was Anton's best friend. At least I assumed he was, considering he was Anton's best man."

"Anton never mentioned anyone named Jeffrey to me," Malie said. "I know that seems odd, but there were a lot of things Anton and I never spoke about. It was just easier that way."

The three men seemed to be having a serious conversation. I couldn't be certain what they were discussing, but it seemed to be of a contentious nature based on the fierce expressions on their faces and their wild arm movements.

"Who is the other man with them?" I asked. This man had his back to me, but somehow he seemed familiar.

"Never seen him before in my life," Malie answered.

I studied the men. Almost everyone was gathered on the patio near the pool or on the lawn, just beyond the pool, but this trio was standing well away from the crowd.

"I feel like I've seen him before. Could he have been at the luau?" I asked.

"Maybe. Pono . . ." Malie turned and interrupted the conversation Pono and Zak were having. "See the man talking to Kingsley? Was he at the luau?"

"You mean Jeffrey?" Pono asked.

"No, the other man," Malie clarified.

Pono studied him. "I don't recognize him, although if he was a friend of Anton's, he might have come later. I left shortly after Anton and I argued, so I was long gone before most of the guests arrived. Why do you ask?"

"Zoe thought he seemed familiar."

As I continued to watch the men, a fourth one walked up. When he turned around, I gasped.

"That's odd," Pono commented.

"The man on the boat," I blurted.

"Yeah, I think you're right," Zak agreed.

The fourth man was definitely the one I'd seen with the gun, and the other man was most likely the one who had been standing next to him. I realized that these men might very well be the kidnappers. We'd seen them on Monday as we were leaving Kahoʻolawe. Judge Gregor had mentioned that the kidnappers had brought them food every few days. We'd rescued the men on Thursday, and the kidnappers had been there just that morning, so it made sense that the previous delivery would have been on Monday.

"Let's remember that we have no idea why the men were on the boat that afternoon," Zak cautioned. "Just because we felt threatened by them, it doesn't mean they intended any sort of harm. They may simply have been taking a pleasure cruise."

"In three-piece suits?" I asked.

"It *was* hot to be out in suits," Malie agreed. "And they were miles away from Oahu or anywhere else other than Kahoʻolawe."

"I bet they were making the supply delivery," I said. "We need to get in contact with Judge Gregor and ask him what the men who brought the supplies usually wore."

"Why would the kidnappers wear suits?" Pono asked.

The man facing us must have noticed us watching them because he said something and the other three men turned to look at us. I could feel the man I knew as Jeffrey glare at us. They were too far away to actually make eye contact with us, but I had a feeling a warning had been implied.

"Do you think Leia knows anything?" I asked as I forced myself to look away.

"Like what?" Pono wondered.

"She must know Jeffrey pretty well if he was Anton's best friend, and I'm sure she must have had reason to interact with Kingsley. If Anton's death and the kidnapping of the three men are related, maybe she overheard something."

"I spoke briefly to Leia on the morning of the luau," Pono said. "She told me that Anton had never mentioned Jeffrey until the day he arrived for the party. She was hurt that he'd never talked to her about the man he cared enough about to make him his best man."

Odd, but that jived with what Malie said about Anton being secretive.

"As for Kingsley, I think Anton was careful to keep his work life and his personal life separate."

"Here come Keoke and Leia," Zak noted.

Keoke came from the house, with Leia following behind him. She looked like a lost soul in a dress that was at least a size too large.

"She's lost a lot of weight in just a few days," Pono commented.

Leia sat on a chair behind the spot that was outfitted with a microphone. She looked straight ahead, but it was hard to tell exactly what she was focused on because she was wearing dark glasses.

"Thank you for coming," Keoke began. He gave a brief speech in which he talked about what a great man Anton had been and how much he'd be missed, and then he invited everyone to help themselves to the refreshments that had been provided. Leia returned to the house without saying a word.

"Go talk to your sister," I encouraged him. "The poor thing looks broken."

Pono hesitated.

"I know you and Anton didn't get along, but did you and your sister have a good relationship before Anton came into the picture?" I asked.

"Yes. We were always very close, but after our parents died, we became even closer."

"Then go talk to her. Offer her comfort. I'm sure she needs to be with you at a time like this."

I watched as Pono made his way to the house. I hoped I was correct in my assumption that Leia wanted to see him. I didn't know Pono all that well and had never even talked to Leia, but deep in my gut, I knew that Leia needed her big brother.

"I see a couple of friends over by the bar," Malie said after Pono left. "Meet up with you later?"

"Absolutely. Go have fun," I encouraged. "So Mr. Zimmerman . . ." I turned to face Zak and put my arms around his waist. "What would you like to do now?"

Zak grinned.

I slapped him playfully. "Not that. Should we attempt to mingle? Go for a walk? Get some food?"

"It looks like Keoke is coming this way," Zak pointed out. "We'll say hi and then maybe get some food."

"I'm so happy you made it." Keoke walked up and stood next to Zak. The men slapped each other on the back, the way men do in greeting. Then Keoke hugged me.

"How is Leia?" I asked.

"As well as can be expected. This has obviously been very hard on her, but she is a strong woman. I'm sure she will be fine once she's had time to grieve."

"This has been difficult for your entire family," I sympathized.

"Are your grandparents here?" Zak asked.

"No. This whole thing has been very hard on them. I'm sure that if Leia asked, they would have come, but we talked about it and decided that we didn't want to do anything that might cause them additional stress. I was glad to see you managed to convince Pono and Malie to come today," Keoke added. "I know Leia is anxious to speak to Pono. She tried calling him, but he wouldn't return her phone calls."

I frowned. Pono had made it sound like *she'd* never contacted *him*.

"I really should mingle, but how about we get together and catch up later tonight? Maybe we can have a drink after the others have gone. You are planning to stay over?" Keoke asked.

"We brought our overnight bags," I answered.

"Excellent. Enjoy the day and we will talk later."

"So about that food . . ." Zak began.

We walked over to the dining tent, where long tables were filled to overflowing with every type of traditional Hawaiian fare imaginable. It was hard to decide where to start, but after much consideration, I decided to take a bite of everything so that I could sample the wide array of offerings. After filling our plates, Zak and I went in search of an empty table. We were lucky to find a table for four squeezed in between two larger tables, each of which sat eight. Zak seemed to know the two men already sitting there and quickly entered into a conversation about fishing. I wasn't interested and didn't recognize the people at either of the other tables nearby, so I began to eavesdrop rather than attempt to join in.

"It's a shame what happened to Anton," a woman in a red sundress was saying to the other seven women at her table. "Poor Leia looks like death. And that dress she had on looked like something she found in a secondhand store."

"Leia is having a rough time at the moment, but I have to say I'm not unhappy she didn't end up married to that man," a woman in a yellow hat responded.

"That's a terrible thing to say," came from a woman holding a teacup poodle.

"I wasn't trying to imply that I was happy that Anton was murdered," Yellow Hat defended herself, "only that I feel it is fortunate Anton and Leia didn't end up married. Poor Luke has been a mess since the engagement."

Luke? I made a mental note to find out more about this Luke.

"If Luke was so broken up about Leia and Anton, why isn't he here today?" Red Dress asked.

"His uncle Brian is still missing, and I know he was staying with his aunt," Yellow Hat said. "She's pregnant, you know. Poor thing, about to have her first baby and her husband turns up missing."

They must be referring to Brian Boxer. I assumed Luke was not only Leia's old flame but Brian's nephew as well. Interesting.

"You know I'm not one to gossip," a lady in a purple blouse added, "but I overheard the woman from the deli telling the woman from the bakery on Second Street that the missing men hadn't really had a boating accident but were being held for ransom by members of a drug cartel from South America."

"Why would a drug cartel be interested in Brian and the judge?" the woman holding the poodle asked.

"Brian is an attorney," Purple Blouse pointed out. "Maybe he was responsible for convicting one of the cartel members."

"Brian is an environmental attorney, not a prosecutor," Poodle Lady corrected her. "If the men Brian went sailing with are being held for ransom, it is much more likely that the kidnapping has to do with some big development."

"Maybe we should ask Keoke about it," Red Dress suggested. "He seems to have his finger on the pulse of any development happening in the Islands. If anyone would know what is going on, it would be him."

"I heard that Anton asked Keoke to invest in his latest project, but Keoke turned him down," the woman holding the teacup poodle said. "I don't think the two men really got along, although Keoke isn't one to make his feelings known, if you know what I mean."

"I do know what you mean," Yellow Hat replied. "And it makes sense that Keoke and Anton might not get along. Keoke and Luke are good friends. Have been for a long time. I think Keoke hoped Leia would marry Luke, and then she went and got engaged to some man she'd known for two minutes. It would never have worked out in the long run. I don't know what Leia was thinking."

"Anton was a good-looking man. And he was rich," Purple Blouse pointed out.

"Oh, posh." Yellow Hat snickered. "A man like Anton could never keep Leia satisfied. Luke is a much better man."

"I do feel bad for Luke," Red Hat said.

"As you should." Yellow Hat nodded. "The poor man has been pining after Leia for years, and based on the amount of time they'd been spending together, it looked like Leia might actually be starting to return his affection. Luke was devastated when Anton swooped in from nowhere and swept Leia off her feet."

"It seems that there may be more going on than meets the eye," Poodle Lady said.

"Some people are saying that Keoke . . ." Red Dress lowered her voice as she began to speak.

"So what do you think?" Zak asked me, interrupting my snooping at what I was sure was a key point in the conversation.

I looked at Zak and frowned. I hadn't been listening to a word the men at our table were saying, so I had no idea what he was asking. All three men were staring at me like they expected an answer of some sort.

"Sailing? Tomorrow?" Zak clarified.

"I guess I should check with Levi and Ellie. I did leave Charlie with them," I reminded him.

"Guess we'll have to let you know," he informed the men.

By the time I'd tuned back in to their conversation, the women were talking about some fund-raiser that was scheduled to take place the following month. I'd give quite a lot to know how that sentence had ended. Some people are saying that Keoke *what*?

Chapter 17

One of these days, I'm going to start listening to that little voice in my head that warns me that my current inclination might not be the best overall strategy. Apparently, however, tonight wasn't going to be that night. Not that it hadn't been a perfectly lovely day. We'd dined on the best food money could buy, watched a fantastic fireworks show over the ocean after dark, and spent a fun-filled day talking to the new friends we'd met thanks to Zak's extroverted nature. I was exhausted by the time we'd finally made it to bed and should have slept soundly but ended up tossing and turning as minutes turned to hours.

I finally decided to get up at 2:13. How do I know that it was precisely 2:13? Because I glanced at the digital clock beside the bed as I quietly unwrapped myself from Zak's arms and pulled on a robe. I tried to tell myself that my only intention was to make my way to the kitchen with the idea of procuring a glass of water, but even as I silently opened the door leading to the hallway and tiptoed into the silent corridor, I knew in my heart that the tossing and turning I'd been experiencing all night was due to an overactive mind.

Judge Gregor, Brian Boxer, and Trenton Baldwin had been kidnapped and led to believe that there were additional captives in other locations. The men seemed to think that whatever was going to happen to them would occur on Monday, after the new judge handed down his verdict on the injunction Judge Gregor had issued in the first place.

Anton seemed the most likely to benefit from the change in decision, but he was dead. He'd been murdered by someone at the luau Zak's friend Keoke had thrown to celebrate Anton's engagement to Leia, Pono's sister. Pono was the prime suspect because he'd not only helped Keoke to prepare the pig but had argued with Anton on the day of the murder and disappeared shortly thereafter. He was also the individual responsible for bringing forward the injunction in the first place.

In my mind, everything seemed to come back to Pono or Keoke, or both. I didn't want to believe that either man was responsible for the events of the past few weeks, but I realized that I needed to quell my curiosity about a statement Zak had made: Keoke was an investor. He invested money, big money, in projects like Anton's. If he had invested in the project—and I had to keep in mind that I didn't have any actual knowledge of that at this point—then Keoke stood to lose a lot of money if the injunction wasn't overturned.

Desperate men have been known to take desperate measures.

I walked down the hall as quietly as my bare feet would allow. The house was dark and I didn't hear evidence of any other late-night insomniacs. I carefully made my way down the stairs to the first floor. My intention, I realized, even if I still clung to the lie I'd told myself about needing a drink of water, was not to quench my thirst but to get a look at Keoke's office.

I hoped there wasn't some sort of alarm system that was going to announce to the world that once again Zoe Donovan was sticking her nose where it didn't belong. I hated to think of Zak's disappointment in me if he were ever to find out that I suspected our host, his friend, of such heinous crimes.

I tiptoed quietly across the living-room floor, then paused briefly to decide which hallway to take. One ventured toward the front of the house, while the other led to rooms at the rear. I had no way to determine which closed door could be Keoke's office and I hated to start opening doors, especially should one or more lead to bedrooms with sleeping occupants.

If this were my house and I was going to select a room to use as a home office, I'd select a room with a view. Based on what I could work out in my head based on the layout of the property and the proximity of the house to the ocean, I was fairly certain that the hallway to the left would afford the best views. Now, to figure out which of the three doors to open . . . The room to the right would be an interior room, while the one on the left should have ocean views. The room at the end of the hall, however, should have the best views of all.

The room was dark and I didn't want to turn on any lights that could alert anyone else who might be awake to my presence. I scooted across the room toward the window as I tried to avoid stubbing a toe on the hardwood furniture. I'd been correct in my assumption about the view; it was spectacular. I turned from the window and scooted back toward the desk. I was preparing to shuffle through the paperwork piled on one side when I heard voices in the hallway. I frantically looked around for a place to hide as two men paused outside the door. At first I couldn't make out anything they were saying, but then I figured out they were talking about someone being missing.

I ducked under the desk, which, in retrospect, was a ridiculous place to hide. If one of the men in the hall was Keoke and he came in the room to get something from his desk, he couldn't help but notice me curled up in the space where his feet would normally rest.

My heart thundered in my chest and my breath grew heavy as I waited for the men to either come in and discover my presence or, much better, leave. After what seemed like hours but was most likely only a few minutes, I heard footsteps retreating down the hallway.

The smart thing to do at this point would be to sneak back to the bedroom Zak and I were using before anyone discovered my presence in Keoke's private space. Of course, no one has ever accused me of going for the smart thing, so I crawled out from under the desk and began sorting through the files as I'd originally intended.

There were files for several different projects Keoke was working on, none of which looked to be the one Anton wanted to build. I began walking around the room, attempting to open file cabinets that were, naturally, locked. I should have realized that if Keoke was mixed up in Anton's mess, he wouldn't leave evidence sitting out in plain sight for anyone to stumble upon.

I tried the desk drawers but found those inaccessible as well. I'd pretty much decided to head back to my room when I heard voices in the hallway again. This time I ducked behind a bookshelf that was set at an angle in the corner of the room. For once, I was grateful I was small.

"I told you I had nothing to do with it." Keoke walked into the room with Anton's friend Jeffrey on his heels.

"The only people who knew about the location were you, me, Jimmy, Queenie, and Kingsley. Jimmy and Queenie swear it wasn't them and I know it wasn't me, so that just leaves you," Jeffrey asserted.

Keoke sighed. I peeked around the corner of the cabinet to see if I could make out whether there was anyone else in the room. Keoke looked stressed as he appeared to be formulating an answer. "We both know that I realize what is at stake," Keoke tried to reassure the man. "Do you really think I'd do anything to put the people I love the most at risk? There has to be another explanation."

I noticed that Jeffrey had a gun in his hand. He extended his arm to point it at Keoke, and for the first time since I'd met him, I noticed the tattoo. "Kingsley thinks you were too soft to do what needed to be done. He thinks you waffled at the last minute and let the men go."

Let the men go. They must have realized that Judge Gregor and the others were no longer in the bunker.

"I didn't let them go, but I should have," Keoke spat. "This whole thing has gotten totally out of hand. I never should have let it happen. Anton is dead, my grandparents are being held captive, we put three men in a bunker where they could have died, and for what? Money? I want you and your goons out of my house."

"We ain't going nowhere. Anton made promises he couldn't keep, and you know what happened to him."

"If you are going to shoot me then shoot me," Keoke said.

Jeffrey laughed. "I'm not going to shoot you. Much too easy. If you don't do what I tell you, I will torture and then kill your precious grandparents. We have a deal and I expect you to uphold your end of it."

Keoke sat down at his desk. He put his head on his arms, which he'd folded on the hardwood. It seemed that I hadn't been wrong after all in my assumption that Keoke was involved; what I hadn't known was whether he'd been a willing participant or merely a pawn.

"What do you want me to do?" Keoke surrendered.

"Gregor and the others are no longer in the bunker, but they haven't returned home either, and there isn't any chatter about them being rescued. My guess is that someone moved them. I still think it has to have been you. I know that you were worried about what we'd do with them after the injunction is overturned on Monday. I want the men brought to me by eight o'clock tomorrow morning or Grandma and Grandpa are toast."

"I don't know where they are," Keoke pleaded. "You have to believe me. I haven't left the island all day; you can ask around. I should be able to put together enough eyewitnesses to prove that what I'm telling you is true."

"Even if you didn't leave, it doesn't mean you didn't hire someone to handle it. Maybe those kids you have staying at your guesthouse? We saw them out by the island a few days ago."

"They aren't involved. They've been diving in the area and have found some relics there. That's all, I promise."

"That little one is a real annoying type. A real snoop."

I am not.

"I wouldn't be surprised if she isn't involved in this whole thing somehow," Jeffrey continued. "I saw her sneaking around your grandparents' place and asking a lot of questions on the day of the luau."

I was not *snooping around.* Okay, maybe briefly, after Anton's body was found. But I wasn't obvious about what I was doing, and I wasn't asking a lot of questions. That man is such a liar.

"I wanted to off her right then, but I let you talk me out of it."

Yikes.

"If she and her friends have my bait, you are both going to end up in the pit," Jeffrey warned.

"I invited them to the party as you requested," Keoke said. "They have been on the island all day, and they stayed over as well. There is no way they could have freed the men. Something else must be going on."

"Maybe they let them go yesterday."

"You were there yesterday," Keoke pointed out.

"Maybe they came by after we left."

Keoke took a deep breath. "They are visitors to the Islands. They don't know the kidnapped men. How would they even know to look for and rescue them?"

"Guess you got about six hours to find out."

Jeffrey left the room.

Keoke continued to sit at his desk, looking totally dejected.

So what now? Should I make my presence known? Tell Keoke where he could find the men? They were safe with the police; maybe Keoke could obtain the help of the Honolulu Police Department to help free his grandparents.

On the other hand, maybe I should stay hidden until he left. It did sound like he had been involved in this whole thing on some level from the start. Might he offer to trade my life for that of his grandparents if given the opportunity?

I was leaning toward making my presence known when someone else walked into the office.

Leia?

"You heard?" Keoke asked.

"I heard." Leia sighed. "What are we going to do?"

"Honestly," Keoke said, "I have no idea."

"I'm sorry I got you involved in all of this." Leia began to cry.

"You couldn't have known what was going to happen. You were just trying to help the man you loved."

"I thought I was doing the right thing," Leia sobbed. "Anton put his heart and soul into that project, and then my brother goes and ruins everything for him. Kingsley wasn't happy. I was afraid Anton would be out of a job if I didn't do something. Anton loved his work. It would have killed him to lose it."

"I know." Keoke hugged Leia. "You couldn't have known what would happen."

"Maybe I should have," Leia argued. "I knew Anton didn't play by the rules, and I should have realized that his partner wouldn't either. When Kingsley's goon showed up and announced that he was going to be Anton's best man, I should have known something was up. I should have come to you right away. Maybe if I had, Anton would still be alive."

"Love can make us blind." Keoke tried to comfort Leia. "Anton was a charming man. He had us all fooled. Come on. I'll walk you back upstairs. Try to get some sleep. I'll figure something out."

After Anton and Leia left, I snuck back up the stairs. I needed to tell Zak what I'd heard. The only problem was that I still wasn't certain what it meant. Was Keoke involved? Was Leia? Could either of them be trusted?

Chapter 18

Saturday, July 5

By the time we got back to Maui, the sun was coming up. I hadn't slept at all the previous night and should have been exhausted, but instead I was totally wound up. I put coffee on to brew and then headed down the hallway toward the bedroom. Maybe a swim would wake me up.

Charlie had been sleeping in the living room when we'd arrived home. He was happy to see us but seemed to need to go out desperately, so Zak had volunteered to take him. I was surprised Charlie hadn't slept with Ellie. He didn't normally like to sleep alone, and Ellie had been happy for the company in the past whenever she'd doggie-sat.

As I passed Ellie's bedroom door, the first in the hallway, I noticed that her bed hadn't been slept in. Odd. I continued down the hall and was just passing Levi's room when Ellie walked out from behind the closed door wearing only one of his long T-shirts.

Her jaw dropped open when she saw me standing in the hall. To be honest, I'm not sure which of the two of us was more shocked that we found ourselves in this particularly delicate situation.

"I don't want to talk about it," she said before hurrying into her bedroom and closing the door.

Levi and Ellie? Well, what do you know?

I continued on to my own room and changed into a bikini. By the time I got out to the patio, Zak had returned with Charlie.

"Are the others awake?" Zak asked.

"Not yet," I replied.

"I thought I'd make some coffee. Can I bring you a cup?"

"Thanks; I left some brewing. I'd love a cup with a little milk."

Zak went into the house to get the coffee while I dove into the pool and swam ten laps. By the time I'd pulled myself out of the water and dried off, I felt almost human again. I laid my towel on one of the lounge chairs and sat down on top of it. It was already warm enough to sunbathe.

"Are you feeling okay after your ordeal?" Zak asked as I sipped my coffee.

"I'll live."

Zak reached over to hold my hand as we sat quietly watching the dolphins in the distance. I tried to relax, but I couldn't help but think about the events of the past few hours.

After leaving Keoke's office, I'd returned to our room and filled Zak in on everything I'd heard. He'd called Judge Gregor's contact at the HPD and informed him of the involvement of the men staying at the estate in the kidnapping of Judge Gregor and the others. We'd pretty much decided to stay in our room to wait for reinforcements when we heard a series of quick *pop, pop, pop*s. I recognized the sound as gunfire, and without thinking things through, ran into the hallway before Zak had the chance to stop me.

Keoke was lying on the floor in a pool of blood. It looked like he was dead. The man I recognized as one of the goons from the boat, probably Jimmy or Queenie, had an arm around Malie's throat, while Jeffrey had a gun pointed at Pono and Leia cowered in the corner with her hands over her head.

I can't explain why I did what I did, but the next thing I knew, I'd jumped onto Jeffrey's back, demanding that he drop the gun. I wasn't armed and had no chance of bringing the man to the ground. Luckily, Leia decided to stop being a victim and dove at his legs, throwing him off balance. Jeffrey fell to the ground—on top of me, I might add—giving Zak the opportunity he needed to grab for the gun he'd dropped when Leia tackled him.

The man holding Pono grabbed for his own gun, but Pono was quicker and managed to elbow him in the groin, rendering him quite helpless. By the time the HPD arrived, we'd tied up Jeffrey and his goons and tried to stop the bleeding from Keoke's chest.

It was too early to tell if Keoke would live. He'd been rushed to the hospital, where a dedicated team of doctors was attempting to save his life. He had not awakened as of yet, but we'd been informed that, although he was still in critical condition, he was stable.

Jeffrey, Jimmy, and Queenie had been taken away in handcuffs, and I suspected by now Kingsley had joined them downtown.

Judge Gregor positively identified Jeffrey as one of the men who kidnapped him after being shown a photo of his tattoo. Deciding not to go down with the ship alone, Jeffrey had been talking ever since.

As we'd suspected, the project Anton and Kingsley had hoped to build was at the heart of everything that had happened. It had been Anton's idea in the first place. He'd talked Kingsley into not only signing on but also investing some of his own money. Anton was dating Malie at the time and wrongly had believed he could "handle her" if anyone from her group decided to contest the location of the opulent resort.

When Pono had found the environmental study conducted by Trenton Baldwin and used it to convince Judge Gregor to issue the injunction, Anton knew he was in trouble. It was our belief that Anton had hooked up with Leia as part of a campaign to gain Keoke's financial and political support.

According to what we could find out from Leia, after Kingsley and his men kidnapped the judge and his friends, Keoke threatened to go to the police, which was when Kingsley sent Jeffrey and a couple of other men to Keoke's grandparents' island to keep an eye on everyone, and to make sure no one ruined their plans. When Anton found out Pono was diving in an area in which he might very well be recognized by the goons going back and forth, he tried to warn him off. When he was unsuccessful, he went to Jeffrey to tell him that whatever the cost, he was out of the whole business, and was killed for his efforts. Leia believed he had been placed in the pit to serve as a very public warning to Keoke and anyone else who might be involved that he wasn't a man to mess around with.

"You're probably going to have a bruise where Jeffrey fell on you." Zak kissed my shoulder.

"It'll be worth it."

"Jumping on a man holding a gun isn't the wisest thing you could have done."

"I know."

"You could have been badly hurt or even killed."

"I know."

"If anything were to happen to you . . ."

"I know."

"Although if you hadn't done what you did, who knows how things would have turned out."

I smiled at Zak. He always made me feel special, even when I knew he really wanted to throttle me for almost getting myself killed.

"I guess Judge Gregor and the others can return to their homes and their normal lives now," I said.

"Yeah. It looks like any danger they were in has passed. I heard they arrested the men keeping Keoke's grandparents captive as well. Neither of them were hurt, but it's taken a toll on both of them. I understand they took Keoke's grandfather to the hospital for observation after he complained of chest pains."

"Do you think Keoke will be charged with anything if he lives?"

"It's hard to say. On one hand, he knew about the kidnappings and didn't do anything about them. On the other, he was trying to protect his grandparents from being killed by keeping quiet. I guess it'll depend on how involved he actually was."

Charlie jumped up onto my chair and licked my face. I could see he was happy I was back. I rarely leave him alone for any length of time. Still, I was happy he wasn't at Keoke's estate when everything went down. I don't know what I'd do if he got hurt.

"Do you think that given everything that's happened, we should pack up and head home early?" Zak asked.

"The event at the Maui Ocean Center is this afternoon," I reminded him.

Zak smiled. "I'd forgotten. I guess we can't let all your hard work winning the tickets go to waste. Maybe we should stay through the weekend and fly home on Monday."

"Might as well. I'll be glad to get home, but I'm sorry we won't be able to stay to continue the treasure hunt."

"The reality is that figuring out what they have and what more there is to find could take Pono and Malie years," Zak reminded me. "We'll stay in touch. If they get closer to figuring everything out, we can come back."

"Malie is going to e-mail me some of the stuff she got from her uncle. I figure I can help with the research part of the adventure from Ashton Falls. There's something about that necklace we found that's nagging at me."

"Nagging how?"

"I'm not sure," I admitted. "I have this feeling I've seen it somewhere before."

Chapter 19

Sunday, July 6

"I can't believe we're going home tomorrow," I said as Zak and I walked down the beach hand in hand while Charlie trotted in front of us. The warm evening air wrapped itself around my shoulders like a comforting embrace as the gentle waves of the sea gently rolled into shore, encircling my ankles and bubbling up between my toes.

"Personally, I think I'll be happy to get back to our daily routine," Zak commented as I leaned my head against his strong arm. "The trip has been fun but stressful."

"Yeah, I guess you're right," I admitted. "Maybe you and I can come back sometime when there isn't so much going on. I still have unused gift cards I need to spend. Most don't have expiration dates, and the ones that do are good for a year or more."

"We can come back any time you'd like." Zak stopped to kiss me.

I wrapped my arms around his neck as a tingling sensation worked its way from my lips down my body.

"I think," Zak nibbled on my lower lip, "we need some time," he made his way down to the side of my neck, "alone."

I couldn't agree more.

Charlie barked, breaking the mood. I watched him dig for a sand crab that had burrowed out of his reach. It was comical to watch him dig for the crab only to have it surface somewhere else and then burrow into a new hole. Charlie hopped from hole to hole with little to show for his efforts other than a sandy nose.

"I've enjoyed spending time with Levi and Ellie, but it seems like they're still dealing with issues that have put a damper on the last days of the trip," Zak said as we continued walking. "I thought they were doing better with everything that happened, but it seems like ever since we got back from Keoke's, the tension between them is thick enough to cut with a knife."

"I guess they have some stuff to work out."

I'd tried to talk to Ellie about her night with Levi, but she'd told me quite clearly that it was a mistake and she didn't want to talk about it. Ever. Levi was uncharacteristically close-mouthed as well.

"I've been meaning to tell you that I spoke to Pono earlier. Keoke is doing better, although he's still listed as being in critical but stable condition," Zak informed me. "Pono is hoping they'll be able to move him out of the ICU in a day or two."

"That's wonderful." I wrapped my arm around Zak's waist. "Do you know if he's going to be charged with his part in this whole mess?"

"Pono didn't say. Actually, I don't think he knows. With everything that's happened, there's a lot to sort out. He did mention that once Judge Gregor and the others were freed, the new judge decided to uphold the original decision and continue with the injunction. From what I've been able to figure out, Keoke invested a bundle in the project. It's going to hurt if he can't figure a way out of his current predicament. He could even go to jail."

"And Leia?"

"As far as I know, she didn't do anything illegal. I suppose once everything is sorted out she could be charged as some sort of an accessory because she knew about the kidnappings."

I stopped walking as we came to a rock jetty. The otherwise gentle waves seemed to pick up speed as they approached the rugged barrier. I watched as seawater splashed up and over the embankment. I was ready to go home, but I was going to miss this place.

"I suppose Keoke's fabulous beach house won't be available the next time we come."

"If he's charged with his part in the kidnappings, he could very well lose everything."

"It was fun while it lasted."

"I suppose we could buy a place of our own," Zak said.

"Here? In Hawaii?"

"Sure." Zak shrugged. "Why not? It would be a good investment, and the idea of us having our own tropical getaway is appealing in more ways than one."

Zak ran a finger down my cheek. He slid his hand behind my head and pulled me forward into a deeply erotic kiss. Just when it felt like my knees might buckle, he pulled his head back slightly.

"I think you might be on to something," I gasped. My heart pounded in my chest and suddenly I had an overwhelming urge to return to the house. To our room. To our bed.

"Then we'll start looking," Zak decided.

"I'm afraid buying an oceanfront getaway is more of a *you* thing than a *we* thing; the *me* of the *we* couldn't afford much more than a mat for the entry," I said with a smile.

"I'm sure we can work something out." Zak lifted me up in his arms and walked me out into the water.

"You don't say," I whispered against his lips as I wrapped my arms around Zak's neck and my legs around his waist.

"I've been thinking," Zak gently kissed me between each word as we gently bobbed in the gentle surf.

"Yeah?" I groaned as Zak's kisses dipped lower.

"We make a good team."

"Umm," I moaned.

Zak stopped kissing me and pulled back slightly. He used his finger to tuck my wild hair behind my ear. He got a serious expression on his face as he looked me directly in the eye.

My body began to shiver, not so much from the cold but as a result of the intensity of the moment.

"Zoe Donovan," Zak pulled me into his gaze, "will you marry me?"

RECIPES FOR MAUI MADNESS

Banana Macadamia Nut Muffins

Loco Moco

Super-Easy Kalua Pig

Banana Cheese Pie

Super-Easy Hawaiian Pie

Easy Pineapple Upside-Down Cake

Banana Macadamia Nut Muffins

1¼ cups mashed ripe bananas (about 3 large)
½ cup sugar
¼ cup dark brown sugar, firmly packed
½ cup (1 stick) butter, melted
¼ cup milk
1 large egg
1½ cups flour
1½ tsp. baking soda
¼ tsp. salt
½ tsp. ground nutmeg
½ tsp. cinnamon
2 cups macadamia nuts, toasted, chopped

Preheat oven to 350°F. Grease twelve muffin cups or line with muffin papers. Combine bananas, both sugars, butter, milk and egg in large bowl. Mix in flour, baking soda, and spices. Fold in half of nuts. Divide batter among prepared muffin cups. Sprinkle tops of muffins with remaining macadamia nuts. Bake until muffins are golden brown and tester inserted into center comes out clean, about 25 minutes.

Loco Moco

A traditional loco moco:

Sticky rice
Hamburger patty
Eggs, any style
Brown gravy

This easy sausage variation makes 8 servings:

Minute rice (4 cups rice/4 cups water)
8 Precooked sausage patties
8 eggs, any style (I scramble)

*Sausage gravy:
1 package (16 ounces) ground sausage, browned
6 tbsp. flour, shaken into 4 cups water

(I put water and flour into a plastic container with a
lid and shake until flour is dissolved. Add to browned
sausage. Simmer and stir until it thickens.)

Salt, pepper, and chili powder to taste

Place ⅛ rice on a plate. Layer on sausage patty over rice. Layer on 2 eggs. Cover with ⅛ sausage gravy.

(I sometimes garnish with chopped green onions.)

Super-Easy Kalua Pig

1 (6 lbs.) pork butt roast
1½ tbsp. Hawaiian sea salt
1 tbsp. liquid smoke flavoring

Pierce pork all over with a carving fork. Rub salt, then liquid smoke over meat. Place roast in a slow cooker. Cover and cook on low for 16 to 20 hours, turning once during cooking time. Remove meat from slow cooker and shred, adding drippings as needed to moisten.

Banana Cheese Pie

2 large bananas
1 ready-made graham cracker crust (or make your own)
8 oz. cream cheese, softened
1 large box vanilla instant pudding
3 cups milk

1 small container Cool Whip
1 cup macadamia nuts, chopped

Slice bananas into pie crust. Mix cream cheese, pudding, and milk together and let set for 5 minutes. Pour over bananas in piecrust. Spread Cool Whip on top and garnish with macadamia nuts.

Super-Easy Hawaiian Pie

1 can crushed pineapple, undrained (20 oz.)
1 box instant vanilla pudding mix (6 servings)
8 oz. sour cream
1 9-inch graham cracker crust
1 small container Cool Whip
I can sliced pineapple
8 maraschino cherries
½ cup flaked coconut

In a large bowl, combine crushed pineapple with its syrup, dry pudding mix, and sour cream. Mix until well combined. Spoon into pie crust. Frost with Cool Whip and decorate top with pineapple slices and cherries. Sprinkle with coconut.

Cover and chill at least 2 hours before serving.

Easy Pineapple Upside-Down Cake

¼ cup butter or margarine
1 cup packed brown sugar
1 can (20 oz.) pineapple slices in juice, drained, juice reserved
1 jar (6 oz.) maraschino cherries without stems, drained
1 box yellow cake mix, eggs and oil called for on box

Heat oven to 350 degrees. In 9 x 13-inch pan, melt butter in oven. Sprinkle brown sugar evenly over butter. Arrange pineapple slices on brown sugar. Place cherry in center of each pineapple slice and arrange remaining cherries around slices; press gently into brown sugar.

Add enough water to reserved pineapple juice to match liquid called for on cake mix box. Make batter as directed on box, substituting pineapple juice mixture for the water. Pour batter over pineapple and cherries.

Bake 42 to 48 minutes (44 to 53 minutes for dark or nonstick pan) or until toothpick inserted in center comes out clean. Immediately run knife around side of pan to loosen cake. Place heatproof serving plate upside down onto pan; turn plate and pan over. Leave pan over cake 5 minutes so brown sugar topping can drizzle over cake; remove pan. Cool 30 minutes. Serve warm or cool. Store covered in refrigerator.

Books by Kathi Daley

Come for the murder, stay for the romance.
Buy them on Amazon today.

Paradise Lake Series:

Pumpkins in Paradise
Snowmen in Paradise
Bikinis in Paradise

Zoe Donovan Mysteries:

Halloween Hijinks
The Trouble With Turkeys
Christmas Crazy
Cupid's Curse
Big Bunny Bump-off
Beach Blanket Barbie
Maui Madness
Derby Divas – coming July 2014

Road to Christmas Romance:

Road to Christmas Past

Kathi Daley lives with her husband, kids, grandkids, and Bernese mountain dogs in beautiful Lake Tahoe. When she isn't writing, she likes to read (preferably at the beach or by the fire), cook (preferably something with chocolate or cheese), and garden (planting and planning, not weeding). She also enjoys spending time on the water when she's not hiking, biking, or snowshoeing the miles of desolate trails surrounding her home.

Kathi uses the mountain setting in which she lives, along with the animals (wild and domestic) that share her home, as inspiration for her cozy mysteries.

Stay up to date with her newsletter, *The Daley Weekly*. There's a link to sign up on both her Facebook page and her website, or you can access the sign-in sheet at: http://eepurl.com/NRPDf

Visit Kathi:
Facebook at Kathi Daley Books, www.facebook.com/kathidaleybooks
Twitter at Kathi Daley@kathidaley
Webpage www.kathidaley.com
E-mail kathidaley@kathidaley.com

32572970R00118

Made in the USA
Lexington, KY
24 May 2014